I0661591

N.Y. Mercentile Library Association

New York City During the American Revolution

N.Y. Mercentile Library Association

New York City During the American Revolution

ISBN/EAN: 9783337227821

Printed in Europe, USA, Canada, Australia, Japan

Cover: Foto ©Andreas Hilbeck / pixelio.de

More available books at **www.hansebooks.com**

NEW YORK CITY

DURING THE

AMERICAN REVOLUTION.

———

BEING

A COLLECTION OF ORIGINAL PAPERS

(NOW FIRST PUBLISHED)

FROM THE MANUSCRIPTS IN THE POSSESSION OF

THE MERCANTILE LIBRARY ASSOCIATION

OF NEW YORK CITY.

PRIVATELY PRINTED FOR

THE ASSOCIATION.

1861.

PREFACE.

THE accompanying work, which bears for its title "New York City during the American Revolution," may be confidered in fome degree as a free-will offering on the part of the Mercantile Library Affociation to thofe of our Members and Citizens who, by their contributions, have fecured to the Library the poffeffion of thofe Hiftorical Manufcripts and Documents known as the *Tomlinfon Collection.*

It was confidered fitting that thofe whofe liberality had been thus difplayed toward us, fhould themfelves be made partakers of the benefits they had conferred, and no more appropriate way prefented itfelf to thofe who had the matter in charge than publifhing a few of the documents themfelves and putting them in a convenient form for prefervation.

For this purpofe, fuch of the papers have been felected as pertained almoft exclufively to the city of New York. and by means of them, a feries of panoramic views are given of the city, from the Stamp Act Riot in 1765, to the Evacuation by the Britifh in 1783.

During the former part of this time—until September, 1776—the city was the fcene of no ordinary excitement. Patriots and loyalifts dwelt here together, but the lines which diftinguifhed them were faft being drawn. The Britifh foldiers and the Sons of Liberty were mutually exafperating each other, and their feelings could not be wholly kept in check. It was not then, indeed, that the ftruggle againft foreign ufurpation firft commenced in this city. It had been going on for well nigh a century. But it was now taking that determined form which was to lead to victory and independence.

During the laft feven years of the above period, the city was in the occupancy of the Britifh army. The glimpfe that we get of it, at this time, imperfect though it be, has a peculiar intereft. Would that fome truthful record of all that tranfpired here during thefe eventful years might be found and given to the public.

There remains now but to thank thofe who have contributed in any manner to the intereft of the volume. To Mr. Henry B. Dawfon, the Hiftorian, is efpecial credit due for the valuable Introductory Chapter, which embodies a defcription of the moft important localities of New York city and ifland at the time the volume commences; and to the fame gentleman is the reader indebted for, with few exceptions, the hiftorical notes which accompany the feveral papers.

Interefting biographical fketches have been contributed by John L. Curtenius, Efq., of Buffalo, S. S. Purple, M. D., of New York, and Henry T. Drowne, Efq., alfo of this city. To Mr. Drowne we are further indebted for copies of feveral interefting letters written from the city by his grandfather, Dr. Solomon Drowne, of Rhode Ifland, contributed with the moft unaffected modefty and generofity.

To D. T. Valentine, Efq., the invaluable clerk of our Common Council, we are under obligations for the ufe of the map engraved for one of the annual iffues of his "Manual."

The hiftorical ftudent will appreciate the fidelity with

which the original Documents have been followed by
the Printer, as regards the fpelling, punctuation, and
even the manifeft errors, which are retained; while the
general reader will catch the fpirit of the times all
the more faithfully from the very want of artificial
elegance, which thefe unpretending letters and narratives
difplay.

MERCANTILE LIBRARY, CLINTON HALL,
    June 20, 1861.

NOTE.—The "Tomlinfon Collection," from which the materials for this
volume have been drawn, confifts of feveral hundred hiftorical papers relat-
ing chiefly to the American Revolution and events immediately connected
with it. Thefe documents, comprifing public and private correfpondence,
army rolls, orderly books, and other matter of like nature, with appropriate
illuftrations, have been brought together, during feveral years of refearch, by
Mr. Abraham Tomlinfon of this city, with the defign of having them ulti-
mately placed in fome public inftitution.

The whole collection was offered to the Mercantile Library Affociation on
fuch terms that it was thought defirable to fecure it for the infpection and
perufal of its members; and this refult has been accomplifhed through the
liberality of friends of the Affociation. It is propofed, when opportunity
favors, to have the moft interefting portions of the collection arranged in fuch
a manner as that they can be eafily feen and ftudied.

CONTENTS.

INTRODUCTION.

I⊤ is, at all times, an interefting employment to turn over the annals of any community, or to liften to the fimple narrative of events in "the olden time," as it falls from the lips of fome aged inhabitant; and in proportion as that community may have participated in the ftirring events of bygone years, will that employment be productive of pleafure and inftruction.

This general conclufion—at all times true—is peculiarly fo when the annals of the city and county of New York are the fubjects of confideration; and there is no community within the extended boundaries of our country to whofe annals the careful ftudent may turn with greater advantage, o⁻ on whofe patriotic and felf-facrificing actions its children may found a more honeft and commendable pride, than on thofe of that city.

It is, indeed, true that the citizens of New York have ever been peculiarly a mixed people; that their taftes and their habits have ever tended toward the buftling fcenes of trade and commerce, rather than to the more quiet retreats of literature and the fine arts; that to other hands than to thofe of her own fons has New York generally intrufted the unwritten hiftory of her patriotifm and her enterprife, the preparation of her literature, and the eduction of her children; and that, looking at the prefent and the future, rather than at the paft, fhe has ever preffed onward and upward toward that proud pofition which fhe will fome day occupy, as the emporium of the world.

It is equally true, however, that the feveral nationalities and conditions of life which are reprefented in the counting-rooms, the workfhops, and the

2

dwellings in New York—elements which, in themfelves, are often difcordant and antagoniftic—through the operations of an overruling Providence, have become the bafis of her immenfe influence and power.   By the combination of thefe feveral elements, the peculiar features of all have been infenfibly neutralized; while a frefhnefs, and elafticity, and ftrength of character, have been imparted to the newly-formed community, which had not been poffeffed by any of the elements from which it has been produced.   In this manner the undue circumfpection of her Dutch and Englifh and German elements, and the preponderating vivacity of her French and Irifh elements, have mutually exercifed a beneficial influence; while the tact and the executive abilities of the emigrants from New England and Scotland, who have fought homes among her people, have added new ftrength to her enterprife, and increafed intelligence to her tradefmen and her mechanics.

It is alfo true that while the demands of trade have been refpected more, in New York, than the claims of literature and the arts, it is not true that the latter have been entirely difregarded by the merchants and the tradefmen of that city.   The numerous valuable private libraries which grace even the more humble dwellings, as well as thofe of the wealthier citizens, and the well-fuftained public collections—many of them defigned peculiarly for diftinct claffes of the people—all furnifh evidence that, in her leifure, at leaft, New York feeks the companionfhip of thofe, of every age and nation, who have contributed to the wifdom of the prefent generation; and that fhe feeks at their hands a portion, at leaft, of that knowledge which they are ever ready to impart.

Nor is it lefs true, becaufe thofe who have written our hiftories and fchool-books have failed to notice *her*, that New York *has a hiftory*, as glorious in every refpect—and, in many inftances, far more fo—as is that of any other community in this or any other country.   Rhode Ifland and Maryland, juftly proud of their colonial liberality, have claimed honor for the *liberty of confcience* which was cherifhed under their authority; yet in New York, alfo, under the laws of her fatherland, the fame freedom had prevailed from the beginning; and the "fectaries" of Maffachufetts, banifhed by the courts of that colony, and no longer fafe even in Rhode Ifland, and the perfecuted and forrow-ftricken Ifraelites of Portugal, driven from city to city and from country to country, found permanent refting places, and continued protection, and unreftrained freedom only within the bounds of her jurifdiction. As early as October, 1664, the merchants of New York defied the power of the Government, and demanded a voice and a vote in the adminiftration of the public affairs; and *they never ceafed to lead the oppofition to the Crown* until the final feparation of the colonies from the mother country. In her acquittal of John Peter Zenger, in 1745, fhe eftablifhed and maintained *the firft free prefs;* and, through that powerful inftrumentality, contributed more to the caufe of the American Revolution, than did any other colony, prior to the battle at Concord. In Auguft, 1760, in her protection of the crew of the *Samfon*, and in July, 1764, in her releafe of the four fifhermen, fhe declared her *oppofition to the impreffment of feamen and the right of fearch*, many years before Rhode Ifland, or any other colony, followed her example. In October, 1764, *fhe appointed the firft Committee of Correfpondence*, fix years before Maffachufetts, and nine years before Virginia took any fteps to imitate her example, although both thefe States have claimed the honor of having originated "this great invention," and hiftorians, even in New York, have boldly feconded their pretenfions. While all others of the colonies, in 1764, quailed before the Parliament—admitting the fupremacy of that body, and the duty of the colonies "to yield obedience to an act of Parliament, though erroneous, till repealed"—New York, alone, declared that *fhe would confider a violation of her rights and privileges, even by Parliament, an act of tyranny;* that fhe would "hate and abhor" the power which might inflict it; and, "as foon as fhe became able, *would throw it off*, or, perhaps, try to obtain better terms from fome other power." When the Stamp Act was enacted, in 1765, fhe led the column of oppofition to it; her merchants *organized the Non-importation agreement;* and, among the faithful, they were *the moft faithful* in the execution of its provifions. *The firft blood* which was fhed in defence of the rights of America, flowed from the veins of *her* inhabitants, on the Golden Hill, January 18,

1770, two months before "the Maſſacre" in King ſtreet, Boſton, and five
years and three months before the affair at Lexington. She, alſo, as well as
Boſton and Annapolis, *had a tea-party :* and ſhe, as well as they, ſeaſoned
the waters of her harbor with the taxed tea which the cupidity of the Eaſt
India Company and the inſolence of the Government had attempted to
thruſt into her midſt — differing from Boſton only in doing fearleſsly, in
broad daylight, and without diſguiſes, what the latter had done with timid-
ity, in the darkneſs of night, and in the guiſe of "Mohawks." And, laſtly,
when hoſtilities had been commenced, as will be ſeen in the following pages,
ſhe did not heſitate to take a place in the very front rank of the oppoſition,
or to prove, by the daring of her ſons, her title to that poſition, by *over-
turning the King's authority in that city*, and by eſtabliſhing in its ſtead a
"Committee of One Hundred" of her citizens, long before any ſimilar ſtep
was taken by any other community in the country.

From theſe circumſtances—ſelected from among a multitude of others—
may be judged whether or not New York has a hiſtory which is worthy of
preſervation ; and whether or not the hiſtorians and the makers of ſchool-
books who have diſregarded her patriotiſm, and left it unnoticed, have either
been true to their country, to themſelves, or to the fidelity of hiſtory. At the
ſame time, and from the ſame circumſtances, alſo, let it be determined what
degree of intereſt it is which cluſters around the contents of this volume,
compriſing exact copies of papers which have never before been publiſhed,
and which relate entirely to the ſtirring events of the American Revolution in New York, or to thoſe of the War of the Revolution through
which the independence of the United States was finally eſtabliſhed.

In the earlier part of the period referred to, as will be ſeen by reference
to the map which accompanies the volume, New York was but a village, in
extent, when compared with the populous and extended emporium which
now ſtretches its boundaries to the fartheſt limits of the iſland on which it
ſtands. The ſame "*Broad Way*," it is true, which then marked the courſe
of the "back-bone of the iſland," as far north as where Duane ſtreet now
croſſes it, is ſtill, as it was at that day, the pride of our citizens, their favorite

promenade, and the great centre of their "fhopping" interefts. " *The Bowling Green*," alfo, and the graveyards of Trinity and St. Paul's, the winding and narrow thoroughfares in the lower part of the city, many of them bearing new names, and all of them divefted of the peculiarities which they then poffeffed, and "*the Commons*," now dignified with the name, although but very few of the acceffories, of a "*Park*," remain to remind us of bygone days, and of generations which have alfo departed, leaving not even a connecting link behind.

At the period referred to, the lower extremity of the ifland was occupied with Fort George and its outworks—the latter embracing three baftions, with connecting curtains, extending from Whitehall flip on the fouth-eaft, to the line of the prefent Battery place on the north-weft.

The fort, a rectangular ftone work, ftrengthened with baftions at its angles, was elevated on an artificial mound, about fourteen feet in height, which had been thrown up "at an enormous expenfe;" and its gateway, which fronted "the Bowling Green," was defended by a raveling or covert-port which had been thrown out in front of the fort, toward the city. Within the enclofure of the fort were the Provincial Governor's refidence, a barrack which would accommodate two hundred men, and two powder magazines—the latter of which, from their dampnefs, were entirely ufelefs; and the glacis or counterfcarp on its eaftern and fouthern fronts, as far eaftward as Whitehall ftreet, and fouthward as far as Pearl ftreet, was occupied as gardens for the Governor's ufe.

The armaments of the fort, the raveling, and the line of works on the water line, were mounted *en barbette:* and although upward of one hundred and twenty pieces of artillery were on the ramparts, a diftinguifhed military engineer of that period has informed us that it "feems to have been intended for profit and form rather than for defence, it being entirely expofed to a fire in reverfe and enfilade;" and that although "it carried a refpectfull appearance with it (at a diftance)," the defences on the northern front were, "of themfelves, but bad, this front being command by a piece of ground equal to it at the end of y Bowling Green, its original parade, and formerly in the jurifdiction of the fort. This height is 530 feet from it, and where its principal ftreet commences called the *Broadway*."

Befide the barracks which were within the fort, another, fometimes ufed for a military hofpital, occupied the fouth-eaftern part of the prefent Battery, extending weftward from Whitehall ftreet along the prefent foutherly line of State ftreet; while a third, in which were pofted the troops who haraffed the people fo much at the period under confideration, occupied the northern part of "*the Common*," on the fouthern line of the Chambers ftreet of our day.

Before noticing other portions of the city, as they appeared at that early day, it may be proper to remark, that the ferry to Staten Ifland occupied the fite, at the foot of Whitehall ftreet, which it ftill retains; and that the eaftern part of the Battery, then and many years afterward, was occupied with a pool of water, into which the tide flowed through Whitehall flip.

A ftranger in New York, in 1767, would have feen little to admire in the plan—or, rather, in the entire abfence of any plan—on which the city had been built; and the lower portions of it ftill retain much of that early peculiarity. The unfeemly juxtapofition of fafhionable private refidences, merchants' ftores, lawyers' offices, and mechanics' workfhops—as we would confider it—alfo muft have formed a curious feature, even in its principal ftreets; but, in this refpect, if not in the former, the modern city has effected a radical and permanent change.

Paffing from the gate of Fort George, and leaving the Provincial Secretary's office on his right—on the weftern corner of the Bowling Green and Whitehall ftreet—the ftroller around town of that day had "the Broad Way," with its well-fhaded fidewalks, before him, and all the bufy fcenes which, from the earlieft days, have rendered it famous in the annals of New York.

Next to the glacis of the fort, on the weftern fide of the ftreet, ftood the elegant manfion of Captain Kennedy, of the Royal Navy—a building which, for architectural pretenfions, was rivalled only by the refidence of Mr. Walton, in Queen ftreet, now Franklin fquare. Like the great city of which it ftill forms a part, it has furvived the fhock of revolutions, the demands of commerce, and the fenfelefs thirft for change; and, with two ftories added to its height, it is now known as "*The Washington*," No. 1 Broadway.

Adjoining the refidence of Captain Kennedy was another, then owned by him, and fubfequently purchafed and occupied by the Honorable John Watts, a fon of the gentleman of the fame name who had been a member of the Provincial Council—brother-in-law of Sir John Johnfon, and brother of Major Stephen Watts, whofe gallantry in the fervice of the King, at the battle of Orifkany, is fo well known. This houfe, alfo, furvives the many changes which have been made in Broadway; and, at the prefent time, is occupied for offices.*

Next above Mr. Watts's refidence was that of Robert R. Livingfton, a juftice of the Supreme Court of the colony, the father of Chancellor Livingfton, and one of the moft diftinguifhed of the friends of the popular movements which, a few months earlier, had convulfed the colony. After having been altered in fome of its parts, this building, alfo, is now occupied for offices.

The fourth houfe in the row, on the weftern fide of the way, was that of the Van Courtlandt family—one of the oldeft and moft influential families in the colony; which has given way to a modern-built refidence, now alfo occupied for offices.

Next on his left was the City Arms Tavern, kept by George Burns—the cradle of American liberty, in which even the patriotifm of Fanueil Hall was rocked in the earlieft ftages of its exiftence. In the large rooms on the fecond floor of that building, the belles and beaux of 1767 frequently met and amufed themfelves in "affemblies;" while occafional concerts and lectures and exhibitions of different kinds found quarters in the fame eftablifhment. But other and more important affemblages than thofe of the votaries of pleafure had met within the large room of the City Arms, and made its

---

* This property was fold to Mr. Watts in February, 1792, for £2000 fterling; in 1836, $107,000 was offered for it, and refufed; $93,000 was bid for it in 1836 or 1837; and, about two years ago, it changed hands for $37,500—a fingular inftance of the upward tendency of trade during the paft few years.

name famous for all time to come. Two years before (*October* 31, 1765), "upwards of two hundred principal merchants" of thofe who "traded to Great Britain" had met in council in that room, and had there declared that they would import no more goods from Great Britain while the Stamp Act remained on the ftatute-books. They had alfo, at the fame time, appointed a "*Committee of Correfpondence*," for the purpofe of effecting a union of the feveral colonies—until that time acting without concert in their oppofition to the Government—and thus having there committed the firft overt act of rebellion; and having, at the fame time, laid the foundation of the union of thirteen feparate and difcordant peoples in that room, the merchants of New York had inaugurated the City Arms as the head-quarters of the American Revolution.

The old building, thus rendered famous in the hiftory of America—for many years known as "The Atlantic Garden"—has alfo remained, with but few alterations, until the paft fummer (1860), when it gave way to the demands of commerce, having been torn down to make room for a freight-depot for the Hudfon River Railroad Company.

Meanwhile, on the oppofite fide of "the Broad Way," was the well-known "Bowling Green," fkirted by a double row of trees which extended up the flope of the ftreet nearly as far as Beaver lane (*Morris ftreet*). The fragments of a broken-down fence which appeared, here and there, around the Green, even at that time, bore filent teftimony to the paffer-by, of the audacity of the citizens, in their oppofition to the Stamp Act of 1765; and revealed the fource from whence were drawn fome of the materials for the bonfire in which alfo were confumed the Lieutenant Governor's effigy, as well as his fleighs, carriage, and harneffes, in the celebrated "Stamp-Act Riot" of November 1, 1765.

In the immediate vicinity of "the Bowling Green," in 1767, were alfo eftablifhed other perfons who were prominent in the mercantile, or mechanical, or focial circles of New York. On the weftern fide of the ftreet were George Croffe and Robert Furfyth, "from Ireland," whofe blackfmith fhop, and weekly advertifements—the latter more in keeping with the practice of the prefent day—were equally prominent. C. Wiggins, alfo, with his fhip-joiner's fhop, was an occupant of the weftern fide of the Broad Way; as was Mrs. Steele, in her "King's Arms Tavern," which fhe had removed from the lower end of Broad ftreet, four years before. On the eaftern fide of the ftreet was the York Tavern; and two doors from Beaver ftreet, alfo oppofite the Bowling Green, was the refidence of Sir Edward Pickering, Bart.

Between Beaver lane and the Lutheran Church, in 1767, Broadway was generally occupied with private dwellings; and the promenader, fo far as we have been informed, met nothing of particular moment. "The alley which led to the oyfter pafty" (*Exchange alley*) on his left, and Verlattenberg, or, as it was generally called, Flatten-Barrack ftreet (*Exchange place*), on his right,—as they ftill do, broke the monotony of the fcene.

At fome diftance to the right, from the Broad Way, on the upper fide of Garden ftreet (*Exchange place*), between Broad and Smith (*now William*) ftreets, at the period of which we write, ftood the ancient church-edifice of the "Old" Dutch Church. It was an oblong fquare, with three fides of an octagon on the eaft fide. In the front it had a fquare tower, of fuch large dimenfions, that the confiftory's meetings were held in it, above the entrance. That ancient meeting-houfe remained until 1807, when it was taken down to make room for a new edifice, which, in its turn, was deftroyed, in "the great fire" of December, 1835.

On the corner of what is now known as Rector ftreet (then without a name), ftood the old Lutheran Church, with its curious belfry; and, in its rear—toward the North River—was "the Englifh fchool," which had been eftablifhed and foftered, through a feries of heavy trials, by the Veftry of Trinity Church. Oppofite the Lutheran Church, on the eaftern fide of the Broad Way, ftood the fchool-houfe of W. Elphinftone, one of the moft accomplifhed teachers, of his day, in the city.

Trinity Church, in 1767, occupied the fame fite—furrounded by the me-morials of the departed—as that on which fhe now ftands. Separated from the fidewalk by a painted picket-fence, the modeft ftructure—one hundred and forty-eight feet long by feventy-two in breadth—prefented its femicircu-

3

lar chancel to the ſtreet; while, at its *weſtern* extremity, its ſimple pinnacled
tower and ſteeple roſe one hundred and ſeventy-five feet into the air. Within, this ancient edifice was ornamented beyond any other place of public
worſhip in the city. The head of the chancel was adorned with an altar-
piece; and oppoſite to it, at the other end of the building, was the organ.
The tops of the pillars which ſupported the galleries were decked with the
gilt buſts of angels, winged. From the ceiling were ſuſpended two glaſs
branches, and on the walls hung the arms of Governor Fletcher and ſome
others of its principal benefactors. That building was deſtroyed in the great
fire of 1776; and the ſubſtantial ſtructure which was erected in its place, in
its turn, has given way to the prevailing taſte for change—the magnificent
edifice which is now the pariſh-church of Old Trinity, repreſenting as truly
the ſpirit of the preſent age as the old building firſt referred to did that of
the merchants and the people of New York in 1767.

Immediately in front of Trinity Church, in the olden time as it ſtill does,
Wall ſtreet extended from the Broad Way to the Eaſt River. In the earlier
days of the colony (1653), "*a wall*," or ſtockade, had been erected along
the northern line of this ſtreet, for the protection of the town—giving a name
to the thoroughfare at its baſe; and, although the neceſſity for the preſervation of that wall no longer exiſted, when Governor Dongan adminiſtered the
government, in 1688, portions of it ſtill remained. On its northern ſide,
near the Broad Way, a little back from the ſtreet, in 1767, ſtood the ſtone,
ſteepled meeting-houſe of the Preſbyterian Church, in the pulpit of which
the Rev. Meſſrs. Treat and Rodgers were accuſtomed to preſent the truths
of the goſpel, as defined by the Weſtminſter Aſſembly; and farther down—
on the lower corner of Naſſau ſtreet, where the Cuſtom-houſe now ſtands
—ſtood the City Hall, which ſerved alſo as the Municipal and Colonial
Court-houſe, the Debtors' and County Jail, and the Capitol of the Province.
The former of theſe buildings—the meeting-houſe—after various changes and
reconſtructions,* was removed, with great care, in 1844, and reappeared, in

---

* Built in 1718; enlarged in 1768; rebuilt in 1810; burned in the fall of 1834; and
rebuilt immediately afterward.

its former ftyle, in Wafhington ftreet, Jerfey City, where it ftill ftands, the meeting-houfe of the Firft Prefbyterian Church—a row of fplendid ftores taking the place of the old meeting-houfe; which, fubfequently, have alfo given way to the demands for "offices," and a row of ftill newer buildings, on the fame ground, now furnifh quarters for a hoft of lawyers, bankers, brokers, infurance companies, &c.; the church, meanwhile, occupying a fine new edifice on the corner of Fifth avenue and Weft Eleventh ftreet. The latter of the two—the old City Hall—after having paffed through many changes (the moft important of which was that under the direction of Major L'Enfant, for the reception of the firft Federal Congrefs, under the new Conftitution), was taken down in 1813, to make way for dwellings and ftores, which alfo, in their turn, have given way to the fine building occupied by the Revenue Department of the Government, before referred to.

Proceeding up the Broad Way, from the Trinity Church, the promenader, in 1767, firft paffed King (*now Pine*) ftreet on his right, and Stone (*now Thames*) ftreet on his left—the former extending eaftward from the Broad Way to the Eaft River; the latter weftward from the fame central thoroughfare to the North River, which at that point then flowed on the prefent line of Greenwich ftreet.

Immediately above Stone (*now Thames*) ftreet, on the weft fide of the Broad Way, in 1767, ftood "The King's Arms Tavern"—fo celebrated in the earlier times. It had been erected in the days of Lord Cornbury; and, fubfequently, it had been the manfion of Lieutenant Governor De Lancey—its gray-ftone walls; its narrow, arched windows, reaching to the floor; its rear piazza, overlooking the North River, and affording a fine lounging-place for the officers of the garrifon and the fafhionables of the city; and its cupola, which afforded one of the fineft views of "Old New York," being among the moft prominent points of intereft remembered by the fojourner in the city, at the period of which we write.

Little-Queen (*now Cedar*) ftreet was next paffed on the right, and Little (*alfo Cedar*) ftreet on the left—then extending from the North River on the weft, as at this time, to Smith (*now William*) ftreet on the eaft.

On the fouth fide of Little-Queen ftreet, between the Broad Way and
Naffau ftreet, ftood the "New-Scots' Church," in which the Rev. Doctor
John Mafon at that time preached (a modeft edifice, fixty-five by fifty-four
feet in extent, which had been erected in 1758); and farther down the
fame ftreet, in an open fpace which extended through to King (*now Pine*)
ftreet, ftood the ancient Huguenot Church, "Du St. Efprit," a ftone edifice,
fifty by feventy-feven feet in extent, whofe quaint hipped roof, and circular-
headed windows, and lofty tower, and crowded graveyard, have difappeared
only within a few years.

In the middle of the Broad Way, extending from the centre of the block
between Little (*now Cedar*) ftreet and Crown (*now Liberty*) ftreet to that of
the next block above, was the wooden fhed which had been dignified with the
name of the Ofwego Market; while, cluftered around it—as was, alfo, the
cafe with the immediate vicinities of other market-houfes in the city—were
the ftores of many of the merchants of that period. The hardware ftores
of Gilbert Forbes, the elder, and that of Peter T. Curtenius, on the latter
of which was difplayed as a fign a large gilt "anvil and hammer," the dry-
goods ftore of Mr. Conover, the boarding-houfe of Mr. Kip, and the tavern
kept by Mr. Miller, were among the principal eftablifhments which gave life
to the fcene around this market-houfe; although others were there whofe
owners, with the edifices which they occupied, have paffed away to be for-
ever forgotten.

Crown (*now Liberty*) ftreet extended from oppofite the centre of the
Ofwego Market, on either hand, to the North River on the weft and to
Maiden lane on the eaft—its prefent limits. On the weftern fide of the
Broad Way, it is probable, Crown ftreet was occupied with refidences—
Melanclon Smith, one of the moft prominent members of the bar, refiding
in one of them. On the eaftern fide of the Broad Way Crown ftreet pre-
fented feveral interefting features. On its northern fide, near the Broad
Way, was the fmall, unaffuming frame building which had been erected in
1706, as a meeting-houfe for the Friends' Society, fubfequently a hofpital
during the Revolutionary War, and afterward the feed-ftore of Grant Thor-

burn, whofe recollections ftill intereft the readers of our newfpapers at frequent intervals. Oppofite to this edifice was the felect fchool-houfe of George Murray—probably a member of the "fociety" which met in the neighboring meeting-houfe—where many of the well-known men of a later period received their education. A few doors below Murray's fchool-houfe, on the fouth-eaft corner of Naffau ftreet, ftood the Middle Dutch Church, with its neat portico and painted picket-fence, and fubftantial tower and belfry, and furrounding graveyard, the fcene of that innovation by Rev. Dr. Laidlie, in 1764—a fermon in the Englifh language—which, at the period of which we write, and for many years after, had called out, and continued to call out, the bittereft oppofition of the confervative Knickerbockers of our city. Adjoining the old church edifice, on the fame fide of Crown ftreet, the gloomy fugar-houfe of the Livingftons, erected fome eighty years before, frowned on the paffer-by; and the horrors of which it was the fcene, from 1776 to 1781, might have been readily foretold, had the mutterings of the rifing ftorm, which were apparent to the careful obferver even in 1767, been noted and confidered. The fugar-houfe, with its evidences of fuffering humanity, has paffed away, leaving only a few walking-canes, which have been made from its timbers, as the witneffes of its former exiftence; the old church edifice, ftripped of its picket-fence and its wooden portico, its pulpit and its pews, has become the centre of the vaft poftal bufinefs of this city, and, having been purchafed by the United States, bids fair to give way at an early day to a more commodious and elegant ftructure. Defcending "the Potter-baker's hill," in front of the refidence of Hon. William Smith, to Smith (*now William*) ftreet, and thence to Maiden lane, where it ftill terminates, Crown ftreet, in 1767, was one of the moft important ftreets in the city, forming, as it ftill does, one of the few thoroughfares in the lower part of the city which extended from river to river.

Maiden lane and Courtlandt ftreet, both well known to the citizens of the prefent day, were next paffed, the former extending to the Eaft River, the latter to the North River. At the foot of the former, in the wide fpace which ftill remains there, was "the Fly Market," while the ftairs on the river near by were one of the termini of the Long Island ferry; at the foot of the latter was the ferry to Powle's Hook (*Jersey City*), which still retains the same position. On the King's wharf, on the North River, between Courtlandt and Partition (*now Fulton*) streets, were the arsenal and the royal storehouses.

Dey street on the west side of the Broad Way, and John street opposite to Dey street, are still well known; and in 1767, and for nearly three quarters of a century afterward, they afforded pleasant places of residence for those who thronged the "business streets" of that portion of the city.

On the eastern side of Smith (*now William*) street, between John and Fair (*now Fulton*) street, in 1767, stood a low, wooden building, in the low loft of which a sailmaker had found a workshop. In that humble edifice, which has remained until within a few years, on the same site, the First Baptist Church in this city found its first *public* abiding place; and, at the period of which we write (1767), the First Methodist Church were also enjoying the same peculiar privilege under the same roof. It is a singular fact that the first *public* resting place of two of the principal religious denominations in this city was in the same unpretending sail-loft; while it is not less remarkable that the old structure was permitted to remain to so recent a date.

East from William street, at the period referred to, the John street of to-day was known as Golden Hill street; and there, and in the Fly (*now Pearl street*) between Burling slip and Fly Market (*now Maiden lane*) the spirited contest known as "THE BATTLE OF GOLDEN HILL," in which was shed the first blood of the American Revolution, was fought on the eighteenth of January, 1770, two months before the "massacre" in King street, Boston, and five years and four months before the affair at Lexington.

On the northern side of John street, near the Broad Way, in 1767, was the only theatre which was then in New York. It stood about sixty feet back from the street, with which it was connected by a covered way extending from the sidewalk to the door of the building. It was of wood, "an unsightly object," painted red; and on the seventh of December, 1767, the first season in that edifice was opened with Farquahar's comedy of *The*

Beau's Stratagem and Garrick's *Lethe*, the celebrated "American Company" taking the several characters.*

* The following, a copy of the advertisement of that performance, which appeared in *The New York Mercury*, of the same date, will interest some of my readers :

By Permission of his Excellency the Governor,

By the American COMPANY

At the Theatre, in *John Street*, this present evening, being the 7th instant *December* ; will be presented, *A Comedy*, call'd, the

S T R A T A G E M .

ARCHER, by Mr. HALLAM,
AIMWELL, by Mr. HENRY,
SULLEN, by Mr. TOMLINSON,
FREEMAN, by Mr. MALONE,
FOIGARD, by Mr. ALLYN,
GIBBET, by Mr. WOOLLS,

SCRUB, by Mr. WALL,
BONIFACE, by Mr. DOUGLASS,
DORINDA, by Miss HALLAM,
Lady BOUNTIFULL, by Mrs. HARMAN,
CHERRY, by Miss WAINWRIGHT,
GIPSEY, by Mrs. WALL,

MRS. SULLEN, by Miss CHEER.

An Occasional Epilogue by Mrs. Douglass.

To which will be added, a Dramatic Satire, call'd,

L E T H E .

ÆSOP, by Mr. DOUGLASS,
DRUNKEN MAN, by Mr. HALLAM,
FRENCHMAN, by Mr. ALLYN,
FINE GENTLEMAN, by Mr. WALL,
MERCURY, (with Songs,) by Mr. WOOLLS,

CHARON, by Mr. TOMLINSON,
Mrs. TATTOO, by Mrs. HALLAM,
Mr. TATTOO, by MALONE,
Mrs. RIOT, (with a Song in character,) by Miss WAINWRIGHT.

To begin exactly at Six o'Clock.

Vivant Rex & Regina.

No Person, on any Pretence, whatever, can be admitted behind the scenes.

TICKETS *to be had at the* Bible and Crown, *in* Hanover-Square, *and at Mr.* Hayes's, *at the Area of the Theatre.*

Places in the Boxes, may be taken of Mr. Broadbelt, *at the Stage Door. Ladies will please to send their Servants to keep their Places, at* 4 *o'Clock.*

BOXES 8s.　PIT 5s.　GALLERY 3s.

On the eastern side of Nassau street, near John, was the new meeting-house of the German Reformed Church, of which the Rev. J. M. Kern was the pastor. This old building has survived until within a few years; and many of those who were in business near John street twenty years ago, will recollect the restaurant of Leonard Gosling, with its hundreds of dishes, which, at that time, found accommodation under its roof.

That portion of Gold street of our day which is between John street and Maiden lane, was called "Rutgers' Hill" in 1767; and the large brewery of Anthony Rutgers, jr., at that time occupied the northern corner of that lane and Maiden lane, where the old established house of Wolfe and Bishop so long did business. Eastward from Golden Hill (*now John*) street, our Gold street, at that time (1767) was known as Vandercliff street—after Dirck Vandercliff, whose orchard, many years before, had occupied that locality; and on its northern side, between Golden Hill (*now John*) street, and Fair (*now Fulton*) street, stood the meeting-house of the First Baptist Church, of which the Rev. John Gano was the pastor. It was then a plain, stone edifice, having been enlarged within three years after its first erection, fifty-two by forty-two feet in extent; and it remained there until 1840, when it was torn down, the materials serving as part of those which were taken for the construction of the new meeting-house in which the same church still worships, at the corner of Broome and Elizabeth streets.

Proceeding up the Broad Way from Dey street, the promenader in 1767 next crossed Partition (*now Fulton*) street, extending westward to the North River; or Fair (*also Fulton*) street, which extended eastward only to the present Cliff street.

On the lower corner of Fair and Dutch streets stood the small frame meeting-house of the Moravian Church, which had been erected in 1751; and on the north-eastern corner of Fair and William streets stood the more imposing stone edifice of the North Dutch Church, which still retains its original appearance and is still used by the same body, as in 1767, and for the same objects.

On the upper corner of Partition (*now Fulton*) street and the Broad

Way, in 1767, ftood St. Paul's Chapel, which had been dedicated in October, 1766; and it ftill ftands there, furrounded by its crowded grave-yard, one of the moft interefting of the few landmarks which have been preferved in our city.

Oppofite to St. Paul's Chapel, the road to Bofton—one of the great outlets from the city—branched off from the Broad Way; and the prefent Park Row, and Chatham ftreet, and the Bowery, indicate the general courfe which it took through the fuburbs of the city.

Vefey and Barclay ftreets, named after two rectors of Trinity Church, Robinfon (*now Park Place*), Murray, Warren, Church, and Chapel ftreets, on the weftern fide of the Broad Way, with the edifice of the King's (*now Columbia*) College at the foot of Robinfon ftreet, are too well known to the citizens of New York of the prefent day to need any particular notice in this place. In 1767, thefe ftreets were generally occupied for refidences— John and Martin Cregier being among the number—although David Grim, who has rendered fo much fervice to the ftudent of our local hiftory, difpenfed his ales and his good cheer at the fign of "the Three Tuns" in Chapel ftreet.

On the eaftern fide of the Broad Way, oppofite the ftreets referred to, was the Common—an open ground, which is ftill well known as "The Park." Even at that early day the people had been accuftomed to affemble at that place to exprefs their wifhes. They had rendezvoufed there on the evening of the thirty-firft of October, 1765, and on the following evening preparatory to the celebrated "Stamp Act Riots;" and at the fame place on the following Tuefday, they had reaffembled, *armed*, with the avowed intention to ftorm the Fort in order to obtain poffeffion of the ftamped papers which had been depofited within it. They had alfo met in that place, on the fifteenth of November, 1765, to exprefs their pleafure when Sir Henry Moore had declared that "he had nothing to do with the ftamps;" and in December of the fame year, when the firft ftamped inftrument appeared in New York, the proceffion which bore it proceeded to that place and burned it with the effigies with which it had been accompanied. On the

+

sixth of March, 1766, also, they had affembled there to exprefs their indig-
nation againft the conduct of Lieutenant-Governor Colden in fpiking the
guns in the king's yard and on the Copfey Battery; and in May of the fame
year they had celebrated, at the fame place, with great fpirit, the repeal of
the obnoxious act. On its weftern margin, nearly oppofite Murray ftreet, the
celebrated Liberty-pole was erected in June, 1766; and around its bafe (or
thofe of the poles which, from time to time, had been erected in the place
of thofe which the foldiers had deftroyed) clufter many of the moft romantic
affociations of that interefting era. On the nineteenth of March, 1767, the
fourth pole had been erected on that fpot in honor of "*the King, Pitt,
and Liberty;*" and the colors had floated gaily from its fummit on the birth-
day of the fovereign.

Within the area of this Common, our prefent *Park*, on the very fpot on
which now ftands the City Hall, ftood in 1767 the Poor-houfe, in the rear
of which was a large garden; while on the fpace between that and the
Broad Way, trees were planted. Eaftward from the Poor-houfe ftood the
Prifon, a rectangular ftone building, furmounted with a cupola—a building
which, during the fubfequent war of the Revolution, was occupied by Cunningham, the provoft marfhal, whofe cruelties to the "rebel" prifoners who
were placed under his charge are fo well known. That building, with modern improvements both interior and exterior, ftill retains its place in the
Park, and is known to all our citizens as "The Hall of Records." North
from the Poor-houfe, near the fite which the row of buildings known as
"The New City Hall" more recently occupied, at that time ftood the long
line of barracks which furnifhed quarters for the troops whofe turbulent fpirit
produced fo much confufion in the city, and whofe determination to cut
down "the Liberty-pole" proved fo powerful an element in the movements
of that period.

On the eaftern fide of the road to Bofton, near the corner of Beckman
ftreet, at that time ftood the unfinifhed ftructure of "the New Prefbyterian
Meeting," within whofe walls, on the following New Year's Day, the mef-
fage of the gofpel was firft delivered by the Rev. Dr. Rogers. That build-

ing, alfo, until within a few months, occupied the fame pofition—being the well-known "Brick Church" meeting-houfe in whofe Society the venerable Rev. Dr. Spring ftill retains his paftorate—but the building itfelf has g'ven way to the demands of trade, and has difappeared.

A fhort diftance below Naffau ftreet, in Beekman ftreet, at that time alfo ftood the remains of the old theatre — the third erected in the city of New York—which had been deftroyed by the people during the political troubles which had fwept over New York a few months before; while a fhort diftance above, on the corner of Frankfort and King George (*now North William*) ftreet, ftood the low ftone church edifice of "the Swamp Lutheran Church," a building which is well-remembered by many of the young men of the city.

At the foot of Warren ftreet, extending to the prefent Chambers ftreet, and overlooking the river, was the Vaux Hall, occupied in 1767 by the celebrated Major Thomas James of the Royal Regiment of artillery. It had been occupied by him during the fummer and fall of 1765 ; and, during the riots which greeted the Stamp Act on the firft of November of that year, it had been vifited and ranfacked by the excited populace, as will be feen by reference to the firft of the feries of papers in the following collection. Immediately afterward he had returned to Europe, but he came back to America in the following year, and probably, at the period of which we write, he was again an occupant of the Vaux Hall, as in 1768 he is known to have refided there. At a fubfequent period the property paffed into the hands of Samuel Fraunces—"Black Sam" of local celebrity during the Revolutionary era. Under his aufpices the eftablifhment was opened as a tea-garden, the vifitors to which were received and entertained with all the grace which, many years afterward, fo peculiarly characterized the chief of the *cuifine* in Prefident Wafhington's eftablifhment. After the Revolutionary War this building was ufed as their firft place of meeting for *public* worfhip by the Roman Catholics in this city—the firft appearance of St. Peter's Church now in Barclay ftreet.

North of the Common, on the eaftern fide of the Broad Way, where

A. T. Stewart & Co.'s dry-goods store now stands, in the olden time was
the negro burying-ground; and on the side hill which extended eastward,
descending toward the Little Collect, in the vicinity of Centre and Duane
streets of 1861, was the place which was usually selected for the public execution of criminals. The "Little Collect" referred to, was a low, marshy lake,
bordered on its northern margin by a strip of high, dry ground, which separated it from the Collect, or Fresh water, a larger and deeper lake which occupied the site of the "Tombs" and its vicinity, with an outlet into the North
River along the present line of Canal street. On the dry strip of ground
separating the two Collects before referred to, near the junction of Centre and
Pearl streets of 1861, stood "the Powder-house," or magazine of the city;
and a short distance east from it, near the site occupied by the Five Points,
was a large tan-yard. The negro burying-ground and the gallows, the
powder-house and the tan-yard have all disappeared; and the two lakes
have been filled up, and their outlet arched over, to afford room for the
demands of an extending city.

The Broad Way extended northward no farther than the present Duane
street, immediately north of which, near the spot where the Hospital now
stands, was the Ranelagh, a noted place of resort in the olden time. Still
farther up, near the spot where Grand street now intersects Broadway, stood
the country residence of Mr. Bayard. It occupied a commanding site which
overlooked the upper part of the city, with the intervening valley and the
surrounding country; and the splendid gardens on its southern front, and
the well-shaded drive which led from the mansion to the Bowery lane, which
it entered a short distance above Broome street, rendered it one of the most
delightful of the many elegant suburban residences of that day.

Extending along the margin of the North River from the fort to Murray
street, on the line of Greenwich street, to the upper extremity of the island in
1767 was the "Road to Greenwich," as it was then called, furnishing another
outlet from the city to the northward. Along this road, also, were scattered
the elegant grounds and residences of many of the leading citizens of that
early day—among which were those of Mr. George Harrison, in the vicinity

of Harrifon ftreet; and Mr. Leonard Lifpenard, near Laight ftreet; that of
Abraham Mortier, Efq., the paymafter-general of the royal forces—fince
well known as the old Richmond Hill, in which General Wafhington and
Aaron Burr have both refided, on the fouth-eaft corner of Varick and Charl-
ton ftreets; that of Lady Warren, wife of Admiral Sir Peter Warren—
which ftill remains, furrounded with the fhade-trees of former times, the well-
preferved refidence of Abraham Van Neft, Efq., one of the oldeft merchants of the city, on Charles, Perry, Bleecker, and Fourth ftreets; that of
James Jauncey, Efq., a leading importer of that day, near Bethune ftreet of
our day; that of Colonel William Bayard, another prominent merchant,
which ftood on the line of Horatio ftreet, between Greenwich and Wafhington ftreets; that of Oliver De Lancey, Efq., fubfequently a brigadier-general
in the royal fervice, which ftood near the line of Thirteenth ftreet, weft from
Ninth avenue; that of Colonel Thomas Clarke—"Chelfea"—in which his
fon-in-law, Bifhop Moore, fubfequently refided, and which has remained
until within a few years, on the fouth fide of Weft Twenty-third ftreet, between the Ninth and Tenth avenues; and that of John Morin Scott, Efq.,
one of the moft learned members of the New York bar, and an early "Son
of Liberty," which alfo remained until within a few years, having been
known as "the Hermitage" and "the Temple of Health," on Weft Fortythird ftreet, between the Eighth and Ninth avenues.

On the eaftern fide of the ifland, alfo, the country feats of the principal
citizens of New York, in 1767, were thickly fcattered. Crofling eaftward
from Mr. Scott's feat, the wanderer of 1767 would have ftruck the Eaft
River near Turtle-Bay, near which, fronting on the Bofton road, an exten-
fion of the Bowery lane, was the elegant manfion of the Friend Robert
Murray, whofe venerable lady, in September, 1776, by detaining the Britifh
officers at lunch, rendered fuch efficient fervice to the retreating Americans.

A fhort diftance above Mr. Murray's (near the prefent corner of Firft
Avenue and Fiftieth ftreet) ftood the country-feat of Mr. Beekman, one of
the moft diftinguifhed of the New Yorkers of that day. That houfe, after
ferving as the head-quarters of Generals Howe, Clinton, and Robertfon,

and furnifhing, in its green-houfe, a prifon for the martyr-fpy, Nathan Hale, ftill ftands one of the moft interefting memorials of old New York now in exiftence. Nearer to the city and to the river, was "Rofe Hill," the country-feat of Hon. John Watts, whofe city refidence on Dock ftreet will be referred to hereafter; while in the immediate vicinity, and reached through the fame lane, on the bank of the river near the foot of Eaft Twenty-third ftreet, was the feat of J. Ketteltas.

Near the Bofton road, alfo furrounded with gardens, were the feats of James Duane, Efq., near Gramercy Park, and T. Tiebout, near the Fourth avenue and Eaft Eighteenth ftreet—the former a diftinguifhed member of the bar, and well known in the subfequent hiftory of his country. The country-feat of Petrus Stuyvefant, then on the bank of the river (but near the corner of Eaft Seventeenth ftreet and the Firft avenue as the city now ftands), and communicating with the Bofton road by means of a long, ftraight, clofely-fhaded drive; that of Gerardus Stuyvefant nearer to the road (near the prefent Thirteenth ftreet, between the Second and Third avenues), and that of Nicholas William Stuyvefant, a fine hip-roofed manfion, with a lofty portico, which ftood in Eighth ftreet, between the Firft and Second avenues, were alfo prominent objects in the north-eaftern fuburbs of the city. Still nearer to the city, on the weft fide of the Bofton road, was the feat of Mr. Herrin, and a fhort diftance below it, that of Mr. Dyckman; while the elegant double, brick refidence of Mr. De Lancey, on the eaftern fide of the Bowery lane near the prefent De Lancey ftreet, with its femi-circular gateway, its denfe fhade trees, and its fine gardens in the rear of the houfe, was one of the moft attractive features in that part of the ifland.

On the extreme eaftern front of the city, weftward as far as the Firft avenue, "the Stuyvefant meadows" prefented their dreary furface; and notwithftanding the march of improvements which has characterized the paft fifty years, there are here and there fmall portions of thefe "meadows" ftill preferving nearly their original level, although furrounded by highly valuable improvements on every fide.

In the fouth-eaftern part of the city near Corlaer's Hook, in 1767, were

alfo fcattered feveral fine country-feats, among which were thofe of Mr.
Jones, called "Mount Pitt," on Grand ftreet near Attorney ftreet; that of
Mr. Ackland, on the extremity of the Hook; that of Mr. Byvanck, one of
the principal among the merchants at that period, near the prefent Gouver-
neur flip; Mr. Degrufhe's with its extenfive rope-walk, near the foot of
Montgomery ftreet; and Mr. Henry Rutgers', on the prefent Rutgers Place.

On the Bowery lane, on his way toward the prefent Chatham fquare, the
traveller in 1767 paffed a new and growing part of the city. From Bayard's
lane above Broome ftreet, to Bayard ftreet weft of the Bowery, although it
had been laid out into blocks, the neighborhood appears to have been settled
only on the line of the great thoroughfare; and Elizabeth, and Winne (*now
Mott*), and Ryndert (*now Mulberry*) ftreets, were comparatively uninhabit-
ed. On the eaftern fide of the Bowery, however, it appears to have been
thickly fettled as far down as Divifion ftreet, and eaftward feveral blocks.
There is no doubt, however, that like nearly every other pioneer movement
in all other parts of the city, and at all times, thefe portions of the town
were the places where the working-claffes chiefly refided, although the vicinity of the public flaughter-houfe which then ftood on the corner of Bayard
and Ryndert (*now Mulberry*) ftreets, naturally attracted many of the butchers of that period to that neighborhood.

On the eaft fide of Elizabeth ftreet, between Hefter and St. Nicholas
(*now Canal*) ftreets, ftood a large windmill, its yard extending through to the
Bowery; and on the weft fide of the Bowery lane, between St. Nicholas
and Bayard ftreets, on the fite now occupied by the Old Bowery Theatre,
ftood an old-fafhioned, two-ftory and attic country tavern—"the Bull's
Head"—furrounded by pens for the accommodation of the droves of
cattle, fheep, calves, etc., which were brought there for a market. The
butchers, who lived near by, and the public flaughter-houfe and "the
Bull's Head" being in the fame neighborhood, many of the diftreffing fcenes
which are now prefented in the ftreets of New York were then unknown;
and the butcher boys—not lefs fond of faft driving, probably, than in our
day—found other opportunities, in 1767, than thofe which are now afforded

while carting their fmall ftock from the cattle-market to the diftant flaughter-houfes.

Below "the Bull's Head," on the fame fide of the Bowery lane, at a diftance from the ftreet, but near the corner of the Pell ftreet of our day (not then opened), in 1767 ftood a fmall, two-ftory frame building, which was the fcene of the tragedy of Charlotte Temple, fo well known to our readers; and a portion of the old building, removed to the corner of Pell ftreet, ftill remains, being occupied as a drinking-fhop under the fign of "the Old Tree Houfe."

Befide thefe objects, nothing of fpecial intereft then exifted to attract the attention of the annalift of that period, until the traveller had paffed down the hill which then occupied the fite of the prefent Chatham fquare, and had approached "the Common" to which reference has already been made.

Catherine and Oliver, James, Roofevelt, and Queen (now *Pearl*) ftreets, branched off to the left in 1767, as they ftill do; the firft three extending to the Eaft River, Roofevelt as far as Cherry ftreet, and Queen by its prefent circuitous courfe joining with Hanover fquare, as it was then called, at Wall ftreet.

The fouthern portion of Queen ftreet at the period referred to (1767) was alfo known as "the Fly;" and it was, at that time, one of the principal bufinefs ftreets in the city. In St. George's (now *Franklin*) fquare, Edward Laight then carried on bufinefs as a currier and dealer in hardware; oppofite to whofe ftore the Hon. William Walton refided, in the ftill well-known "Walton Houfe," at that time the moft elegant private refidence in the city. Near the fame ftreet (*Queen or Pearl*), in Peck flip, at that time was the dry-goods ftore of James Farquarfon; while near "the fhip yards" at the foot of James, Oliver, and Catherine ftreets, was the large diftillery of the Defbroffes family. In the fame ftreet (*Queen*) near Beekman, were the watch-makers and jewellers' fhop of T. & M. Perry, and the large mercantile eftablifhment of Walter Franklin, one of the leading merchants of his day. In Beekman ftreet above Cliff, as is ftill the cafe, St. George's Chapel ftood —a folid, but very neat edifice, which had been opened for divine fervice in

1752; and in Beckman flip near Queen ftreet was the extenfive hardware ftore of Hubert Van Wagenan, whofe fign of a "Golden Broad-axe" was fo often referred to in the annals of that period. Further down Queen ftreet, near the Burling flip, was the hardware ftore of William & Uftick, on which were difplayed a large "Lock and Key."

This Uftick was undoubtedly one of the firm of William & Henry Uftick, whofe deliberate violation of the non-importation agreement in March, 1775, among other matters, led to the celebrated meeting of "the Sons of Liberty," at the Liberty-pole on the Common, on the fixth of April, 1775, at which John Lamb and Marinus Willett prefided, and Captain Ifaac Sears—"King Sears"—called on the people to arm, and to fupply themfelves with twenty-four rounds of ammunition; and he was one of the moft influential merchants in the hardware trade of that day.

Oppofite Burling flip, alfo in Queen ftreet, was the eftablifhment of Jacob Le Roy, with its varied affortment of hemp, cordage, yarn, dry goods, hardware, etc.; while juft below the ftreet, in the flip, was the grocery of Jeremiah Brower.

Proceeding down Queen ftreet toward Maiden lane, the large grocery of Peters & Rapelje was paffed; and "the Fly Market," or rather the Fly Markets—for it is faid there were *two* wooden fheds which bore this collective name—foon afterward prefented itfelf to the view of the paffer-by. The Fly Market occupied the flip at the foot of Maiden lane, as already ftated; and there, alfo, were the ferry ftairs at which the boats from Brooklyn difcharged their paffengers and their cargoes.

Around this Fly Market, as around all the other markets of that day, were the refidences or bufinefs eftablifhments of many of the merchants of New York. William Malcolm, one of the early veftrymen of Trinity Church; Mr. Rapelje, a leading importer of the varied merchandife ufed in the colony; Alexander Wilfon, a heavy dealer in dry goods; Philip Livingfton, a dealer in hardware, glafs, grindftones, marble chimney-pieces, rum, furs, etc.—a leading politician, and a figner of the Declaration of Independence, in 1776—near the ferry ftairs; Walter & Thomas Buchanan

5

& Co, dealers in dry goods, cables, fhoes, etc.—to whom the New-York tea
fhip was configned in 1773; McDavitt, the auctioneer; and Nicholas Car-
mer, at the fign of "the Crofs-Handfaws," were among the number of thofe
who did bufinefs there; while Bowne & Rickman, Richard Williamfon,
and Smith Ramadge, large dealers of goods of every conceivable character,
were in Queen ftreet, in the immediate vicinity.

Proceeding thence down Queen ftreet, King (*now Pine*) ftreet was next
paffed—Little Queen (*now Cedar*) ftreet at that time extending down no
farther than Smith (*now William*) ftreet—and near by, the attractive goldfmith's and jeweller's ftore of Charles Oliver Bruff was fure to arreft the
attention.

Wall ftreet alfo was a place of trade in 1767, as well as one of refidences. At that time, among the eftablifhments of other merchants who
were there, might have been feen thofe of Breefe & Huffman, dealers of
dry goods, crockery, etc.; John Allicocke, one of the moft earneft of
the "Sons of Liberty," a dealer in wines, teas, etc., on the corner of Queen
(*now Pearl*) ftreet; Edward Agar, a dealer in drugs, near the City Hall
(*now Cuftom-houfe*); John Thurman, jr., a dealer in dry goods, on the
corner of Smith (*now William*) ftreet; Jofeph Cox, a dealer in upholftery
goods; Samuel Verplanck, a dealer in dry goods; and Mr. Coley, a filver-
fmith, near the Coffee-houfe (*Water ftreet*).

Below Wall ftreet, proceeding down Hanover fquare—Queen ftreet extending only to Wall ftreet—the paffer-by in 1767 entered one of the bufieft
quarters of mercantile New York. Theophilact Bache, Richard Bancker,
and Henry Remfen, jr. & Co., heavy dealers in dry goods; Elizabeth Col-
vil, a leading milliner and dealer in dry goods; Samuel Broom & Co., extenfive dealers in hardware and cutlery, rum, pork, crockery, etc.; Abram
Duryee, dealer in dry goods, paints, oils, etc.; Hugh Gaine and James Rivington, the well-known publifhers and bookfellers; Peter Goelet—a former
partner of Peter T. Curtenius, a member of the popular "Committee of
One Hundred," and grandfather of our refpected fellow-citizen, Peter Goelet, Esq., of Broadway and Eaft Nineteenth ftreet—one of the moft exten-

five dealers in hardware, mufic, brufhes, etc., at the fign of "the Golden Key;" McLean & Treat, dealers in drugs and medicines; Glen & Gregory, dealers in dry goods, nails, wines, etc.; and Henry Wilmot and James Mc-Evers, the latter the well-known ftamp-mafter of 1765, dealers in general merchandife, were among thofe whofe ftores were in that vicinity; while "the Old Slip Market" with its concentration of bufinefs increafed the buftle of the neighborhood.

The Old Slip Market, like the other market-houfes of that day, was only a low wooden fhed; although, like them, it was furrounded, in 1767, with the bufinefs places of the merchants and retailers of the city. Among the former that of Gerardus Duyckinck—"the Univerfal Store"—in which nearly every thing found a place, was the moft confpicuous; although William Beekman at the fame time, like many a merchant in the country now-a-days, offered an extenfive affortment of cables, hemp, broadcloths, etc., etc., for cafh or country produce.

Below the Old Slip, in 1767, Hanover fquare was not known, and our Pearl ftreet, from thence to Whitehall ftreet, was called Dock ftreet. It was a ftreet in which were private refidences as well as places of bufinefs; and there is no doubt that in confequence of its proximity to the two markets in Coenties and Old flips, to the Exchange at the foot of Broad ftreet, and to the Fort, that it was one of the bufieft in the city. In this ftreet, near Whitehall, among others, refided the Honorable John Watts, a member of the Colonial Council, fpeaker of the General Affembly, and, in 1775, the intended fucceffor of Lieutenant Governor Colden in the government of the colony; and Henry Van Vleck, alfo among the moft refpectable men in the city. Among the merchants who tranfacted bufinefs in Dock ftreet were Joris Brinckerhoff, John Erneft, John Morton, and Clarkfon & Sebring, all dealers in general merchandife; Dirck Brinckerhoff, who fold hardware and metals at the fign of "the Golden Lock;" Henry Cuyler, who dealed largely in fugars; and Anthony Van Dam, whofe trade was principally confined to wines and liquors.

In Pearl ftreet near Coenties flip, in 1767, was "the Fifh Market;" and

around that, as a centre, were alfo cluftered many of the mercantile eftablifhments of that period. Abeel & Byvanck, at the fign of "the New York
made Spade and Sithe"—a fignificant fign when the non-importation agreement of 1765 was remembered—fold hardware in that vicinity; and there,
alfo, were John Abeel, who dealed in anchors; and John and Garrett Abeel,
who were falters doing a large bufinefs. John Hammerfley & Co., prominent merchants of that period; Ifaac Low, the Prefident of the Chamber of
Commerce and of the popular "Committee of One Hundred," although,
finally, a loyalift refugee; and Benjamin Booth, dealing in general merchandife, were alfo among thofe who did bufinefs near the Coenties Market. Mr.
Vanduerfon, largely engaged as a tallow-chandler and foap-boiler, as well as
a dealer in watches, mufic, and jewelry, tranfacted his bufinefs in "Bayard
ftreet, near the Coenties Market;" and there, alfo, were the crockery and
glafs ftores of George Ball; the fchool-houfe of Clementina and Jane Fer-
gufon; and the refidence of John Livingfton, Efq.

The river fronts, alfo — efpecially that on the Eaft River — furnifhed
places of bufinefs to many of the merchants and tradesmen of that period.
On Hunter's quay, between Old flip and Wall ftreet, were Grey, Cunningham & Co., dealers in dry goods, boots and fhoes, metals, paints, glafs, hardware, fifh, groceries, rum, etc.; on Rotton row—the weft fide of Old flip,
between Little Dock (now Water) ftreet and Cruger's wharf (Front ftreet)
—were the law-office of John Coggill Knapp, a notorious pettifogger of that
period; the goldfmiths' fhops of John Dawfon and Samuel Tingley; and the
fhip-chandlery of Samuel Loudon—afterward the patriotic printer of "The
New York Packet," whofe fervices during the War of the Revolution are fo
well known to every ftudent of American hiftory; and on Cruger's wharf
(Front ftreet between Old and Coenties flips) were the fhip-chandlery of
Henry White, and the mercantile eftablifhments of John & Thomas
Burling, and William Seaton & Co.; while Abraham Mercier kept a ftock
of hardware at the fign of "the Crofs-keys and Crown," near the Powle's
Hook ferry, at the foot of Courtlandt ftreet, on the North River.

At the period referred to (1767) the city of New York was the head-quarters of the military establishment in North America; and General Thomas Gage, the commander-in-chief of the forces, refided in a large double house, furrounded with elegant gardens, on the fite now occupied by the stores 67 and 69 Broad street.

Among the members of the bar of New York in that day, the principal were the Hon. William Smith, a member of the Council and justice of the Court of King's Bench, who refided on Potter-baker's hill between the Dutch Church and the Fly Market (*Liberty street, between Naffau street and Maiden lane*); John Morin Scott, whose refidence in "Greenwich" has been already referred to; Benjamin Kiffam, from whom at that time Lindley Murray and John Jay were imbibing leffons in law and loyalty to the crown; William Smith, the younger—one of the triumvirate through whose inftrumentality, principally, the revolution in New York had been effected; William Livingston, fubfequently governor of New Jerfey—to fecure whose daughter for his wife John Jay appears to have found a refting-place for his political principles; and Melancton Smith, whose refidence in Crown street has been already alluded to.

As Judge Smith remarked a few years before, at the period of which we write "this city was the metropolis and grand mart of the province, and, by its commodious fituation, commanded alfo all the trade of the weftern part of Connecticut and that of New Jerfey. No feafon prevented her ships from launching into the ocean; and during the greatest feverity of the winter an equal, unreftrained activity ran through all ranks, orders, and employments."

The following table of the exports from the colonies to Great Britain alone, and that which follows it, showing the imports from Great Britain into the fame colonies, exclufive of thofe from Ireland and the other colonies, will show the relative importance of the trade of New York, even at that early period; while to the mercantile reader they will be equally interesting, in other refpects; the latter, efpecially, will illuftrate the fidelity of the merchants of New York to the non-importation agreement of 1765, when compared with that of the merchants in the other colonies.

TABLE OF EXPORTS from the several Colonies in America to GREAT BRITAIN, exclusive of their exports to all other places, from 1700 to 1767.

Year	New England			New York			Pennsylvania			Virginia & Maryland			Carolinas			Georgia		
	£	s.	d.	£	s.	d.	£	s.	d.	£	s.	d.	£	s.	d.	£	s.	d.
1701	32,656	7	2	18,547	3	6	5,220	6	3	235,738	18	4¼	16,973	6	3	...	...	...
1705	22,793	4	8	7,393	1	4	1,309	17	7	116,768	17	8½	2,698	18	0	...	...	...
1710	31,112	17	7	8,203	18	2	1,277	2	7	188,429	8	6	29,793	9	0	...	...	...
1715	66,555	12	8	21,316	19	10	5,461	4	9	174,756	4	6	29,158	0	5	...	...	...
1720	49,206	12	6	16,836	12	7	7,928	14	10	331,482	2	5	62,736	6	8	...	...	...
1725	72,021	12	6	24,976	5	3	11,981	1	3	214,730	2	2	91,942	13	7	...	...	...
1730	54,701	5	10	8,740	11	3	10,582	1	4	346,823	2	3	151,739	17	11	...	...	...
1735	72,809	15	6	14,155	8	2	21,919	6	3	394,995	12	5	145,348	7	11	...	...	...
1740	72,389	16	2	21,498	0	5	15,048	12	3	341,997	10	11	266,560	4	5	3,010	16	11
1745	38,948	10	9	14,083	3	9	10,130	9	2	399,423	6	3	91,847	5	3	924	9	8
1750	48,455	9	0	35,634	8	6	28,191	0	0	508,939	1	10	191,607	6	3	1,942	19	11
1755	59,533	6	11	28,054	12	3	32,336	10	6	489,668	17	10	325,525	13	6	4,437	16	10
1760	37,802	13	1	21,125	0	0	22,754	15	3	504,451	1	11	162,769	6	7	12,198	14	10
1763	74,815	1	9	53,988	14	4	38,228	10	2	642,294	2	9	282,366	3	6	14,469	18	4
1764	88,157	1	9	53,697	10	4	36,258	18	1	559,408	16	1	341,727	12	7	31,325	9	4
1765	145,819	0	1	54,959	18	2	25,148	10	10	505,671	9	9	385,918	12	0	34,183	15	8
1766	141,773	4	11	67,020	11	8	26,851	3	1	461,693	9	4	293,587	7	8	53,074	16	7
1767	128,207	17	4	61,422	18	7	37,641	17	0	437,926	15	0	395,027	10	1	35,856	15	7

TABLE OF IMPORTS into the ſeveral Colonies in America from GREAT BRITAIN, excluſive of their imports from all other places, from 1700 to 1767.

Year.	New England.			New York.			Pennſylvania.			Virginia & Maryland.			Carolinas.			Georgia.		
	£.	s.	d.	£.	s.	d.	£.	s.	d.	£.	s.	d.	£.	s.	d.	£.	s.	d.
1701	86,322	13	11¼	31,910	6	6¾	12,003	16	10	199,683	2	3¼	13,908	8	3½	....		
1705	62,504	0	10½	27,902	14	9½	7,206	10	3½	174,322	17	3¼	19,788	6	8	....		
1710	106,338	6	4	31,475	0	9½	8,594	14	5¼	127,639	0	5¾	19,613	18	11¾	....		
1715	164,650	7	6	54,629	1	5	16,182	7	7	199,274	17	1	16,631	19	1	....		
1720	128,767	2	11	37,397	19	5	24,531	15	2	110,717	17	10	18,290	12	11	....		
1725	201,768	0	4	70,650	8	0	42,209	14	2	195,884	11	6	39,182	12	8	....		
1730	208,196	5	5	64,356	16	6	48,592	7	5	150,931	6	5	64,785	11	5	....		
1735	189,125	5	7	80,405	9	4	48,804	11	4	220,381	6	9	117,837	3	10	12,112	13	2
1740	171,081	2	5	118,777	8	10	56,751	14	9	281,428	10	11	181,821	14	11	3,524	7	7
1745	140,463	4	7	54,957	1	2	54,280	10	11	197,799	12	3	86,815	13	6	939	14	1
1750	343,659	6	8	267,130	0	0	217,713	0	11	349,419	18	3	133,037	0	9	2,125	15	5
1755	341,796	7	3	151,071	5	0	144,456	7	2	285,157	4	5	187,887	4	9	2,630	19	4
1760	599,647	14	8	480,106	3	1	707,998	12	0	605,882	19	5	218,131	7	8	....		
1763	258,854	19	6	238,560	2	1	284,152	16	0	555,391	12	10	250,132	2	0	44,908	19	9
1764	459,765	0	11	515,416	12	1	435,191	14	0	515,192	10	6	305,808	1	6	18,338	2	11
1765	451,299	14	7	382,349	11	1	363,368	17	5	383,224	13	0	334,709	12	8	29,165	16	9
1766	409,642	7	6	330,829	15	8	327,314	5	3	372,548	16	1	296,732	1	4	67,268	5	5
1767	406,081	9	2	417,957	15	5	371,830	8	10	437,628	2	6	244,093	6	0	23,334	14	2

The city of New York, as it appeared in 1767, has been prefented to the reader with all the care and particularity which the circumftances will allow —a defcription which, it is hoped, will enable the reader of the following papers the more completely to underftand their meaning. As the purpofe of that defcription has been fimply to illuftrate the text, and to facilitate the examination of the interefting papers which have found places in this volume, by the general reader, there has been no defire to do more than to render the peculiar features of New York in 1767 as diftinctly as poffible, leaving to each individual reader the ufe of the material which has thus been furnifhed, in fuch manner and in fuch connection as his own tafte may determine, as he pro-greffes with his work. If, in this fingle defire, the purpofe of the Editor may be followed by fuccefs; if the readers of the following papers fhall thereby be led to take any greater intereft in their contents, or to feel any ftronger regard for the general fubject on which they treat, or to look back with any greater degree of pride on the hiftory of the city which was the fcene of the feveral events referred to, the labor which has been beftowed on this chapter will not have been fpent in vain, and one of the moft agreeable rewards which can attend the ftudent of American hiftory, will have been the lot of the writer.   H. B. D.

Morrisania, N. Y., *April* 13, 1861.

NEW YORK

AMERICAN REVOLUTION.

LETTER DESCRIBING THE STAMP ACT RIOT IN NEW YORK.

[The following letter, written from the city of New York on the day after the celebrated Stamp Act riot, gives an interesting account of that event —not always strictly accurate, it is true, but tolerably correct in the main.

The Stamp Act was enacted in March, 1765, to take effect throughout the colonies on the first of November in that year; and in every part of America the most intense excitement prevailed. Among the opponents of the measure there had been none so energetic or so fearless as the colony of New York; and the merchants of the city of New York appear to have resisted the measure with the greatest determination.

On the evening of the 31st of October, a meeting of the merchants " trading to Great Britain" had been convened at Burns' City Arms Tavern; and they had resolved to import no more goods from the mother country while the Stamp Act remained in force. At the same time they had appointed a *Committee of Correspondence* to organize the opposition, and to secure concert of action among the colonies, *many years before the appointment of any similar Committee in any other colony*—the Committee appointed by the General Assembly of New York, on the 18th of October, 1764, having alone preceded it.

On the evening of the eventful 1st of November, the riot occurred which is described in this letter; and so energetically was the opposition maintained that the act was repealed in the following May.

Other particulars of this momentous event may be found in Lieutenant

6

Governor Colden's defpatches to Secretary Conway, on the 5th of November, 1765, and to the Lords of Trade, December 6, 1765; HOLT's *New York Gazette or Weekly Poftboy*, No. 1192, November 7, 1765; EDES & GILL's *Bofton Gazette*, November 11, 1765; *The Bofton Poftboy and Advertifer*, November 11, 1765; Dunlap's "Hiftory of New York," I., p. 419; Bancroft's "United States," V., pp. 355–6; Graham's "Hiftory of America," (*London edit.*,) IV., pp. 233–4; Ramfay's "American Revolution," I., pp. 65, 66; Booth's "Hiftory of New York," pp 418–420; Dawfon's "Sons of Liberty in New York," pp. 82–111.]

NEW YORK *Nov* 2nd 1765

Dear Sir

      I Have Receiv'd my Cheft and your Letter With the Greateft Pleafure immaginable, and am Extreamly Gladd to Hear that you are well   I had the Good Luck to get on Board a Sloop from Claverack, but did not Get fo Far as N. Winfor[1] till the fecond night About 2 OClock then the wind Halld to the N W and we went thro the way Gat[2] like hell out of A Great Gun—A fea Term—and Got to N York about 11 the Next day   I m now in A Good ftate of Health for which I thank my God and I Hope You may Receive thefe in the fame ——

      I m juft now in high fpirits full of Old Madiera and will Give you A View of the Sons of America[3] by whofe Refentments will or would ftamp the drummer[4] had he not

[1] "*New Windfor*," two miles below Newburgh.

[2] "*Way Gate*"—one of the narrow paffes in the Highlands, through which the Hudfon river flows.

[3] Probably intended for "the Sons of Liberty"—an affociation organized for the purpofe of refifting the aggreffions of the government in the colonies.

[4] A nickname which had been applied to Lieutenant Governor Colden.

Given A Proclamation to the Mob that he'd have nothing to do with them' —— ——

The firſt day of Novʳ our City ſeem'd to be Very much diſturbd but did not ſay much by Reaſon that they did not know wether the ſtamps took place the firſt or ſecond day² the firſt Evening there raiſ'd A Wonderfull Large Mob but Did no damage by Reaſon of the uncertainty³ the 2nd

---

¹ One of the placards through which this determination was conveyed to the people can be ſeen in the fine collection of papers belonging to the New York Hiſtorical Society. It is in theſe words :

"THE LIEUTENANT GOVERNOR declares he will do nothing in Relation to the STAMPS, but leave it to Sir HENRY MOORE to do as he pleaſes on his arrival. Council Chamber, New York, Nov. 2, 1765.

"By order of his Honour,

"GW. BANYAR, D. Cl. Con.

"The Governor acquainted Judge *Livingſton*, the Mayor, Mr. *Beverly Robinſon*, and Mr. *John Stevens*, this Morning, being Monday the 4th of November, that he would not iſſue, nor ſuffer to be iſſued, any of the STAMPS now in Fort George.

"*Robert R. Livingſton*,
"*John Cruger*,
"*Beverly Robinſon*,
"*John Stevens*.

"The Freemen, Freeholders, and Inhabitants of this City, being ſatiſfied that the STAMPS are not to be iſſued, are determined to keep the Peace of the City at all Events, except they ſhould have other Cauſe of Complaint."

² This ſtatement is entirely erroneous, and can only be accounted for in the fact that the writer was a ſtranger in the city ; the date is alſo contradicted by the date of the letter itſelf (*Nov.* 2d). *All the contemporary authorities* except this, which I have met with, agree that the great riot occurred on the evening of the *firſt* of November.

³ The demonſtration here referred to, occurred on the evening of Octo-

Day we heard that the Governor was defign'd to diftribute the ftamps[1] he fent for the foldiers from tortife bay[2] he Planted the Canon Againft the City[3] he fixt the Cowhorns with mufket balls 2 Cannon was Planted Againft the Fort Gate for fear the Mob fhould Break in, Loded with Grape fhot, he ordered the Canon of the Batery[4] to Be fpiked up for the Mob fhould Come fo far as Break out A Civil war And nock down the fort Major James[5] had faid never fear for I drive N York with 500 Artilery Soldiers[6] he Placed Soldiers at the Gaol[7] to Prevent the Mobs Letting out the Prifoners   he Orderd 15 Artilery Soldiers at his

ber 31, as will be feen by reference to HOLT's *New York Gazette*, No. 1192, Nov. 7, 1765.

[1] In this, alfo, the fame error of date occurs. If there was any fpecial report on this fubject at all, it was on the *firft* inftead of the *fecond* of November, as may be feen by a reference to any of the contemporary authorities.

[2] This force had probably been moved into the fort in compliance with a requeft from Lieutenant Governor Colden to General Gage, September 2, 1765.

[3] See alfo HOLT's *New York Gazette*, 1192, November 7, 1765.

[4] This refers to the guns on the Copfey Battery, near the foot of Whitehall ftreet, which had been fpiked by order of the Lieutenant Governor to prevent the people from turning them on the fort. This very act, however, increafed the excitement of the times, and at a fubfequent period called forth feveral popular demonftrations, particulars of which may be found in "*The Park and its Vicinity*," (*Valentine's Corporation Manual* for 1855, pp. 440–442.)

[5] Major Thomas James of the Royal Artillery.

[6] The remarks of Major James, on which this ftatement was bafed, have been differently interpreted ; and a fynopfis of the difcuffion can be found in "*The Sons of Liberty in New York*," pp. 83, 84.

[7] The prefent "Hall of Records" in the Park.

house Near the Coledge[2] where Black ſam[1] Formerly dwelled and the reſt of the ſoldiers he kept in the fort in readineſs for an Ingagement In the Evening the Citizens begin to muſter about the ſtreats About 7 in the Evening I heard A Great Hozaing Near the broadway I ran that way with a Number of Others where the Mob juſt began they had an Ephogy of the Governor[4] made of Paper which ſat on An old Chair which A Seaman Carried Upon his head the Mob went from the Fields[5] down the Fly[6] hozaing at Every Corner with Anumber light of Candles the Mob went from thence to Mr. Macivers[7] who was appointed for ſtamp Maſter in London Since he did not

[1] This houſe, known as Vaux Hall, ſtood near the ſone of the river, ſurrounded by taſtefully arranged grounds, on the block formed by Warren, Chambers, and Greenwich ſtreets, and Weſt Broadway.

[2] King's, ſince called Columbia College, at the foot of Park place, a building which has given place to the three of ſeveral of the members of this Aſſociation within a few years.

[3] Samuel Fraunces, a ſwarthy man, well known in the city at that time as a public caterer, and ſubſequently as the ſtreward of the culinary ſtaff of Preſident Washington.

[4] "Ephogy of the Governor." See alſo, Holt's No. 1146 Gazette, of the November 7, 1765; Lieutenant Governor Colden's deſpatch, November 6, 1765; and Boſs & Gain's New York Gazette, November 11, 1765.

[5] Now known as "The Park."

[6] Pearl ſtreet below Beekman was then known as "The Fly," from the marſhy margin of the river, by the ſide of which it extended. Vide De Voe's MS. "Market Book," volume I.

[7] James McEvers, the gentleman who had received the appointment of ſtamp-maſter, and who reſigned it at the requeſt of the people, lived on the ſpot where the building in Wall ſtreet, now ſtands. His place of buſineſs was in Hanover ſquare.

Except it they Honor'd him with 3 Hozaurs[1] from thence
they went to the fort[2] that the Governor might fee his
Ephogy if he dare fho his face   the Mob gave feveral who-
zaus and thretened the Officers upon the wall Particularly
Major james[3] for faying he'd drive N York with 500 Men
Now tis faid that the Governor was A Drummer in the
Army at Scotland[4]   the Mob had Affurance Enough to
break open the Governors Coatch houfe and took his
Coatch from under the muffle of•the Canon   they Put the
Ephogy upon the Coatch   one fat up for Coatchman with
the Whip in his hand whilft Others drawed it About the
town,   down to the Coffy Houfe[5] the Merchants was Ex-

[1] "*Three huzzas*."

[2] Fort George, at the foot of Broadway.

[3] "*Major James*"—Thomas James received a captain's commiffion in
the Royal Artillery, March 1, 1755, and a major's, October 23, 1761.   In
the fall of 1765 he had come down from Crown Point; and had halted two
companies of artillery, then in the city, on their way from England to the
North, to affift in enforcing the Stamp Act in New York, the refult of which
is feen in this letter.   He was promoted to a lieutenant coloneley, January 1,
1771; to a colonel's command, February 19, 1779; and to the poft of
colonel commandant of the artillery, July 6, 1780.   His firft wife, a Spanifh lady, died in 1776;- his fecond was Margaret, daughter of James De
Peyfter, Efq., of Jamaica, New York, who furvived him.   Mrs. Martin, his
daughter, died in New York in Auguft, 1835.

[4] Referring to a report prevalent at that time, which has been denied,
however, that Lieutenant Governor Colden had been a drummer in the
army of the Pretender, in Scotland, many years before.

[5] *The Merchants' Coffee Houfe*—a noted place of refort at that time—
ftood where the *Journal of Commerce* office now ftands, at the corner of
Wall and Water ftreets.

ceidingly Pleaf'd And the mob Still increafing from
thence ❋ ❋ ❋ ❋ ❋ ❋

❋ ❋ ❋

with About 5 or 600 Candles to alight them   it was a dark
night and not A Breath of Wind   I ran down to the Fort
to hear what they faid   as the Mob Came down' it made A
Butifull Appearance And as foon As Major james faw them
I haar'd him fay from off the wals—Hear they Come by
G—d As foon As the Mob fee the fort they Gave three
Chears and Came down to the Fort   they went under the
Cannon which was planted A Gainft them with Grape fhot,
they bid a Soldier upon the wals, to tell the rebel drummer
or Major James to Give orders to fire[2]   they Placed the
Gallows Againft the fort Gate and took Clubs and beat A
Gainft it[3] And there Gave three Whozaus in defyance   they
then Concluded to Burn thefe Ephogys and the Governors

[1] "*The mob came down.*" After the Lieutenant Governor's coach and
fleighs had been taken from his carriage-houfe, they were dragged through
the ftreets toward the Common—now the Park—by the party which had
feized them; and, while on its way, this party met another then on its way
to the Fort, united with it, and moved "down" Broadway in the manner
defcribed in the letter.

[2] In an anonymous notice which was pofted at the coffee-houfe during
the day, fimilar defiance had been iffued; and Lieutenant Governor Colden
had been threatened with fummary punifhment fhould he "fire upon the
town."

[3] ——"they intrepidly marched with the Gallows, Coach, &c., up to
the very Gate, where *they knocked and demanded admittance*, and if they
had not been reftrained by fome humane Perfons who had Influence over
them, would doubtlefs have taken the Fort."—Holt's *New York Gazette*,
1192, November 7, 1765.

Coatch in the Boldengren¹ before there Eyes² they told M
James as foon As the Coatch was burnt they would knock
down his houfe   then they *   *   *   *

    *   *   *   *   *   *

was juft going to Major James to Knock his houfe down
and if he was A Man he fhould Go and defend it.   the
Ladys fainted as they Could not Go on board———
Then the Mob Gave three Chairs and went to Major Jameſes
And drove the Soldiers out the Back way   then with one
Confent they began upon the houfe and in Lefs than 10
Minutes had the windows and dores the Looking Glaffes
Mehogany Tables Silk Curtains A Libiry of Books all the
China and furniture   they feather Beds they cut and threw
about the ftreets and burnt broke and tore the Garden drank
3 or 4 Pipes of wine deſtroyd the Beef throo the butter
about and at Laft burnt the whole³ only one red Silk Cur-
tain they kept for A Colour⁴   then they diſtroyed the   The
3 day they was refolv'd to have the Governor Ded or Alive⁵

---

¹ The Bowling Green—ftill preferved, at the foot of Breadway.

² ——"we make no Doubt, the L——t G——r, and his Friends, had
the Mortification of viewing the whole Proceeding from the Ramparts of the
Fort."—EDES & GILL's *Bofton Gazette*, November 11, 1765.

³ As a partial compenfation for this damage Major James received four
hundred guineas in England; and, in December, 1766, the Affembly of New
York voted him a gratuity of £1745 15s. 2d., as a further compenfation.
Vide Journal of Affembly.

⁴ As "the Colours of the Royal Regiment, were taken out and carried off
triumphantly"—(*Vide* HOLT's *New York Gazette*, 1192, November 7, 1765)
—there is no doubt the writer here refers to that circumftance.

⁵ "The next day letters and Meffages were fent unto me, threatening my

The fort Got up the fathiens[1] in order for Battle And the mob began before dark the Governor fent for His Councel which held about 2 Hours whilft thoufands ftood by ready waiting for the word the Gov[r] concluded and promifed faithfully to have nothing to do with the ftamps[2] and he would fend them back to London with Capt Davis[3] * * * all Peacable all the mob went home every man to his home * * Britons

E CARTHER[4]

---

life, if I did not deliver up ftamped papers."—*Lieut. Gov. Colden to the Lords of Trade*, 6 Decr, 1765.

[1] "*Fafcines*"—long bundles of fticks and brufhwood, which are ufed for filling up ditches, erecting breaftworks, etc. In this cafe they were probably defigned to form fhelters for the troops who were required to defend the parapets of the fort.

[2] *Vide* Note 1, page 43.

[3] Capt. Davis, of the *Edward*, on which the Stamps had been brought to America.

[4] Owing to the fignature being blotted, the name of the writer of this homely but picturefque epiftle cannot be made out with entire certainty.

7

NEW YORK IN 1770.

EXTRACT FROM A LETTER OF BENJ. YOUNG PRIME.

[The letter from which the following has been extracted, is a bufinefs letter which was written from the city of New York to Dr. Petrus Tappan, of Efopus (*now Kingjton, Ulfter County, N. Y.*). It clearly indicates the difficulties which " the Sons of Liberty" in New York had to encounter in the ftruggle of the American Revolution, and the character of the agencies which the government appealed to in fupport of its prerogatives.

The troubles which arofe from the hand-bill call for a public meeting, to take into confideration the betrayal of the popular rights by the General Affembly of the province (together with copies of the call itfelf, of the fecond hand-bill figned " *Legion*," and of other documents which this affair produced,) have been fully defcribed in Dawfon's " The Park and its Vicinity" (*Valentine's Manual* for 1855, pp. 446–449); and Leake's " Life of General John Lamb," pp. 49–63.]

NEW YORK, April 12th, 1770.

SIR,

     ※   ※   ※   ※

Capt McDougal[1] is indeed in Jail, & I hope if he is

---

[1] Subfequently General Alexander McDougal of the army of the Revolution. He had been arrefted on the information of James Parker, the printer of it, on a charge of writing the hand-bill call of the meeting, figned " *A Son of Liberty;*" and having refufed to give bail, he had been thrown into prifon. " Captain McDougal" was a wealthy retired fhipmafter, an active " Son of Liberty," and a fincere patriot. After the war, he was the firft prefident of the Bank of New York, and he died in 1795.

brought to tryal, he will come off with flying colours[1]. The party againſt him is very virulent &, I hope, impotent. I myſelf am threaten'd (by papers thrown into my houſe) with a Damnation Drubbing and Impriſonment, on ſuſpicion of being the Author of the *Watchman*[2]. So that for 4 or 5 Weeks paſt I've walk'd the Streets (eſpecially of an Evening) arm'd with either a Sword or Piſtols or both. No attempt however has been made upon me, except the night the firſt letter was thrown in, when (as my Servᵗ tells me) a Man knock'd at my door, dreſſed in a flapp'd hat over clubb'd hair, a Watch-Coat, a Ruffled Shirt & a pair of Sailor's Trouſers. A pretty kind of Diſguiſe indeed! I'm likewiſe accuſ'd by one of the papers thrown into my houſe of being the Author of the Paper ſign'd *Legion*[3];

---

[1] He does not appear to have been tried, although the grand jury returned a true bill againſt him at the April term of the court.

[2] A ſeries of political eſſays which appeared about that time.

[3] The following is a copy of this paper, taken from the original in the library of the New York Hiſtorical Society :—

"TO THE PUBLIC.

"The Spirit of the times renders it neceſſary for the inhabitants of this city to convene, in order effectually to avert the deſtructive conſequences of the late BASE INGLORIOUS conduct of our General Aſſembly, who have in oppoſition to the loud and general voice of their conſtituents, the dictates of ſound policy, the ties of gratitude, and the glorious ſtruggle we have engaged in for our invaluable birthrights, dared to vote ſupplies to the troops without the leaſt ſhadow of a pretext for their pernicious grant. The moſt eligible place will be in the Fields, near Mr. De La Montaigne's and the time,—between 10 and 11 o'clock this morning, where we doubt not every friend of his country will attend.

"LEGION."

tho' God knows I'm not the Author of the one paper or the other. You fee, & I hope you will in your Town properly reprefent, the Conduct of the party oppof'd to us.

In cafe of a new Election I hope you will exert yourfelf fo far as your Influence extends & fo far as your Connections will admit, to procure the Election of fuch Members as you can believe will prove friends to their Country. If I'm not miftaken, I've heard that Mr. Clinton has Marry'd your Sifter[1]. If fo, I give you joy! He's a *very* good man: but I'm afraid he has been overfeen in voting againft my Friend McDougal. i. e. in joining in the Vote, that the paper fignd *A Son of Liberty*[2] was a Libel: whoever it might be that wrote it.   *   *   *   *   *
         *   *

Sir,

Your humble Servt,

BENJ. YOUNG PRIME.

Addreffed
    "To Dr. Petrus Tappen
         at Eufopus."

[1] George Clinton, afterward Governor of the State, married Mifs Cornelia Tappan, fifter of Dr. Petrus Tappan, to whom this letter was addreffed.

[2] A copy of the hand-bill addreffed "To THE BETRAYED Inhabitants of the City and Colony of NEW YORK," and figned "A Son of Liberty," may be found in *Valentine's Manual* for 1855, pp. 482–484.

COLONEL MARINUS WILLETT'S NARRATIVE.

[The fubſtance of the following narrative has been publiſhed, by the ſon of the diſtinguiſhed author of it, many years ago, but in confequence of the rarity of that publication, and the intereſt which attaches to the fubject and its author, it has been confidered expedient to prefent the ſtatement in the form in which Colonel Willett left it. Hiſtorical ſtudents will underſtand the great value of this verſion of the narrative, when compared with the fummary publiſhed in 1831; and they will prefer it, even while the latter may be on their ſhelves; while thofe who do not poffefs that publication will the more heart-ily welcome the narrative in its prefent form.

Colonel Marinus Willett, the writer of this narrative, was born at Jamaica, Long Iſland, July 31, 1740. In 1758 he joined the army under General Abercrombie, as a lieutenant in Colonel De Lancey's regiment; was in the difaſtrous action near Ticonderoga; and accompanied Bradſtreet in his expedi-tion againſt Fort Frontenac.

He was one of the earlieſt friends of freedom in New York; and as a member of "*The Sons of Liberty*," was an active participant in the oppoſi-tion to the government—an inſtance of which is related in this narrative.

Accepting a captain's command in the Firſt New York regiment, com-manded by Colonel McDougal, he was with Montgomery in the Northern campaign of 1775–6.

In the fpring of 1777 he was promoted to a lieutenant colonelcy, and commanded Fort Conſtitution, on the Hudſon. At Fort Stanwix, in the Mohawk valley, he performed one of the moſt fignal exploits of the war; and he remained in command of that poſt until the fpring of 1778, when he joined the main army under Waſhington, with which he was prefent in the action at Monmouth, June 28, 1778.

He was with Sullivan in his campaign againſt the Indians; and in 1780, 1781, and 1782, he was actively engaged in the valley of the Mohawk, ren-dering great ſervice to his country.

In 1792 Prefident Waſhington appointed him to treat with the Creek In-dians; and in the fame year he was appointed a brigadier general in the army

defigned to operate againſt the North-weſtern Indians, which office he declined.

He was ſheriff of the county of New York from 1784 to 1787, and from
1791 to 1795; and mayor of the city in 1807.

In the ſecond war with Great Britain he alſo joined with great ſpirit; and
on the 22d of Auguſt, 1830, he died, aged 90 years.]

The account of the Lexington Battle[1] was received at
New York the Sunday after it took place[2] and occaſioned
an Impulſe in the Inhabitants which produced a general
Inſurrection of the Populace who aſſemblyed and not being
able to procure the Key of an arſnell[3] where a number of
arms belonging to the Coloniel Goverment were depoſited
forced open the door and took poſſeſſion of thoſe arms con-
ſiſting of about 600 Muſkets with Bayonets & Catrige
boxes to each filled with ball Catridges[4] Theſe arms were
diſtributed among the moſt active of the Citizens who formed
themſelves into a Voluntary Corps and aſſumed the Gover-

[1] This "account," ſigned by " *T. Palmer, One of the Committee of
Safety,*" dated " *Watertown, Wedneſday morning, near ten o'clock, April
19, 1775,*" can be found entire, in *The New York Gazette and Mercury,*
April 24, 1775.

[2] " This city was alarmed yeſterday by a report from the eaſtward, that
the King's troops had attacked the Maſſachuſetts-Bay people."—*Letter from
New York to a gentleman in Philadelphia,* April 24, 1775.

[3] " *The Arſenal*" here referred to was a portion of the City Hall in Wall
ſtreet, in which the arms of the city were kept.—Leake's "*Life of General
Lamb,*" p. 103.

[4] " Towards evening (*Sunday, April* 23,) they went and ſecured about
half the city arms; a guard of about one hundred men, I am told, was then
placed at the City Hall, to ſecure the reſt of the arms."—*Letter from New
York,* April 24, 1775.

ment of the City. They poffeffed themfelves of the keys of the Cuftome-houfe and took poffeftion of all the public ftores.[1] There was a general ftagnation of bufinefs. The armed Citizens were Conftantly parading about the City Without any Definate object. Part of the 18th Britifh regiment called the Royal Irifh under the Command of the Major of the regiment[2] who were garrifoned in the City Confined themfelves to their barraks.[3] The unfyftemifed and Confufed manner in which things were conducted manifefted the neceffity of forming fome regular plan of Goverment to effect which a meeting of the Citizens were requefted at the Merchants Coffee-houfe when it was Unanimoufly agreed that the Goverment fhould be placed in the hands of a Committee and folemn refolutions Entered into to Support their meafures untill further provifion fhould be made by the Continental Congrefs[4] which were

[1] "Lamb and Sears then returned to the cuftom-houfe, demanded the keys of the collector, and having received them, they difmiffed the officers and clofed the building; fending notices to Philadelphia and elfewhere of what they had done, and calling upon all good patriots to follow their example." —Leake's " *Life of General Lamb*," p. 102.

[2] The major commanding the detachment of the Royal Irifh regiment here referred to, was *Ifaac Hamilton*. Mr. Loffing (*Field Book, II.*, p. 588) fays Major Moncreiffe commanded, but a reference to Lieut. Gov. Colden's defpatch to Earl of Dartmouth, May 3, 1775, will difprove that ftatement.

[3] The Barracks were in "the Fields"—as the Park was then called—occupying a place on a line with Chambers ftreet, near the fite lately occupied by "the New City Hall."

[4] The Continental Congrefs met at Philadelphia, on Wednefday, May 10, 1775.

shortly to meet in Phyladelphia. The seacred honor of the
Citizens being pledged at the same time to support the
measures of Congress. This Committee amount to 100[1]
was Instantly Choosen and entering with becoming deliberation on the duties Delagated to them restored as much
order in the city as under circumstances so new and ex-
troordinary could be reasonably expected[2]—It is proper

[1] The following gentlemen constituted this "*Committee of One Hundred*,"
as it was called: Isaac Low, *Chairman;* John Jay, Petr V. B Living-
ston, Philip Livingston, Isaac Sears, David Johnson, James Duane, Alexr
McDougal, John Broom, John Alsop, Thomas Randall, Leonard Lispenard,
William Walton, Joseph Hallett, Gabriel H. Ludlow, Nicholas Hoffman,
Abraham Walton, Henry Remsen, Petr Van Schaack, Peter T. Curtenius,
Joseph Bull, Abraham Brasher, Abraham P Lott, Abraham Duryee, Francis
Lewis, Joseph Totten, Thomas Ivers, Hercules Mulligam, John Anthony,
Francis Bassett, Victor Bicker, Theophilus Antony, John White, William
Goforth, William Denning, Isaac Roosevelt, Jacob. Van. Voorhees, Jeremiah
Platt, Comfort Sands, Robert Benson, Willm W. Gilbert, John Berrien,
Gabriel. W. Ludlow, Nicholas Roosevelt, Frede Jay, Edward Fleming,
Lawrence Embree, Samuel Jones, John Delancey, William W. Ludlow,
John B Moore, Rudolphus Ritzema, Lindley Murray, John Lasher, Lan-
caster Burling, George Janaway, James Beekman, Samuel Verplanck, Richard
Yates, David Clarkson, Thomas Smith, James Desbrosses, Eleazer Miller,
Augustus Van Horn, Garrat Keteltas, John Read, Benjamin Kissam, John
Moran Scott, Peter Goelet, Cornelius Clopper, John Van Cortlandt, John
Marston, Jacobus Van Zandt, Gerardus Dyckman, John Morton, Thomas
Marston, George Folliot, Jacobus Lefferts, Richard Sharp, Hamilton Young,
William Seton, Abraham Brinkerhoff, Benjamin Helme, Robert Ray, Wal-
ter Franklin, David Beekman, Evert Banker, Michls Bogert, William
Laight, Samuel Broom, John Lamb, Daniel Phœnix, Anthony Van Dam,
Daniel Dunscomb, John Imlay, Oliver Templeton, Lewis Pintard, Cornelius
P Low, Petrus Byvank, Thomas Buchannan. [*London Papers*, XLV.]

[2] "You will not be surprised to hear that congresses and committees are
now established in this Province, and are acting with all the confidence and

here to obferve that the City of New York Contained a
very larg portion of perfonal Influence in favour of the
meafures of the Britifh Goverment and many of the perfons choafen on the Committee were of that defcription[1].
The very ftrong Current of popolar Influence however
which pervaded as foon as advife of the affair at Lexington arrived keept that Influence in fufficient Check
while its tendency to Lengthen deliberation was not without ufe and opperated more powerfully in fupport of the
doings of the Committee—The Britifh troops Garifoned
in the city were Ordered to Join the army at Bofton. It
would have been an eafy bufinefs to made them prifoners.
The timid difpofition of the Committee Caufed them to
fuppofe this could not be effected without the lofs of a
number of lives, and agreed to let them depart with their
arms and acoutraments without Moleftation. They accordingly marched from the barracks to embark about Ten
oClock in the forenoon of a fine pleafant day[2]   There was
a public houfe near Beekman Slip keept by a Mr Jafper
Drake[3]. At this houfe the warm friends of the oppofition to
the Britifh meafures ufed to meet dayly. I was at that place
with about half dozen more when word was brought that the

authority of a legal government."—*Lieut. Gov. Colden to Earl of Dartmouth, 7 June,* 1775 (Colden MSS. New York Hiftorical Society's Library).

[1] A very large proportion of " the Committee of One Hundred," as well as
the "Committee of Fifty," which fucceeded it, were friends of government.

[2] June 6, 1775.—*Lt. Gov. Colden to Earl of Dartmouth, June* 7.

[3] *Vide* page 61.

8

troops had Commenced their march. And that befide the
arms and acoutraments they carried they were taking with
them fundry Carts Loaded with Chefts filled with arms—As
we were among the number of thofe who confider the per-
miting the troops to depart at any rate when we had it in
our power to make them Prifoners proceeded from fear
or fomething worfe and as the permiffion given by the
Committee did not extend to their taking any fpare arms
with them It was fuddenly determin to hazard the Confequence of endeavouring to feizee upon thefe fpare arms.
The perfons prefent by agreement fet out on different routs
through the City to alarm our friends. My rout led me to
pafs the Coffee-houfe[1] where after notifying the meafure
about to be purfued I proceeded through Water Street to
the Exchange which then ftood at the Lower End of Broad
ftreet from whence I difcovered the Troops on their March
down Broad Street I proceeded up the ftreet and on difcov-
ering feveral Carts Loaded with Chefts of arms in front of
the troops under a fmall Guard I ftopt the front Horfe
which of Courfe caufed a halt in the whole line of march.
On the appearance of the Commanding officer to Enquire
into the caufe of the halt I informed him that the permiffion of the Committee did not extend to the troops taking
with them any other arms than thofe they carried about
them—The appearance of David Mathews who had lately

---

[1] Corner of Wall and Water ftreets, on the fite now occupied by the office
of the *Journal of Commerce*.

been appointed Mayor of the City[1] (and whofe tory principals were well known to be oppofed to Congerfenal meafures) diverted the Converfation from the Commanding officer of the troops to himfelf—The halt of the troops afforded time for the Collection of the Citizens. The Carts loaded with arms were turned out of the line of march, And the troops under arms addreffed with an Invitation to fuch as difliked the Service in which they were to recover their arms And receive the protection of the Citizens who confidered them as Bretheren of the fame famaly But if their fentiments corobarated with the Violent meafures of the Britifh Goverment and they were difpofed to Join in the Barbarous work of fheding the blood of their fellow citizens we were ready to meet them in the Crimfon field. One of the Soldiers recovering his arms was received with repeated huzzas and Led away by the Exulting citizens, fome few afterwards followed and were Conducted with the taken arms to a place of Safty[2]. The troops marched to the river and embarked under the Hiffes of the citizens[3].

[1] Colonel Willett's memory had failed to render good fervice in this inftance. Whitehead Hicks—at the period referred to, and until February, 1776—was the mayor of the city; and David Matthews, in April and May, 1775, was alderman of the Eaft Ward, in which capacity he *may* have been prefent.

[2] To the ball-alley and yard of Abraham Van Dyck, corner of Broadway and John ftreet, as will appear from the accompanying ftatement, page 55.

[3] " General Gage wrote to Major Hamilton, by the Afia, that he thought it would be a proper meafure to put the Troops under his command on Board of that Ship, and defired him to confult with me upon it. As I was very

[The following lines, also taken from the autograph of Colonel Willett, appear to have been part of another version of "*the Broad street affair.*" Although there are many particulars which have appeared in the preceding narrative, there are, also, some which are not related in that; and it has been considered proper to publish both, rather than to mutilate either of them.]

The particulars attending this transaction will I trust Justify the account I shall give of it: Similar sensations with those

sensible this small number of Troops (*one hundred*) could not be of any use in the Barracks, and were exposed to those very disagreeable circumstances I have already mentioned, I did not doubt of the propriety of the measure proposed by Genl Gage a difficulty however arose on account of the women and Children, who were too numerous to be taken on Board with the men, almost the whole that belong to the Regiment being in the Barracks here with this detachment. This occasioned a delay of eight or ten days in which time several soldiers deserted. We at length thought of enchamping the Women and Children on what is called the Governors Island, till they could be otherwise taken care of, and yesterday was fixed for embarking the Troops on Board the Afia. The Provincial Congress had notice, that some people proposed to stop the embarkation upon which they published a hand Bill advising the People by no means to molest the Troops, or interrupt them in their design. They likewise appointed a number of their members to join the City Magistrates and assist them in preventing any interruption to the Troops. As soon as the Troops marched from the Barracks, several People began to harangue them, exhorting them to desert, and assuring them of sufficient Protection. Two or three fellows had the hardiness to turn off with their arms, from the Ranks, and were immediately carried away by the People, when the Troops got upon the Dock where they were to embark on board of Boats, the Carts following in the rear with their Baggage, were stoppd and in the Face of the Mayor, Aldermen, Congress and Committee men, turn'd about by a few desperate fellows, carried to a Place in Town, where they opened the Baggage, and took out a number of spare arms and all the ammunition belonging to the Detachment. The Troops embarkd without their Baggage."—*Lt. Gov. Colden to the Earl of Dartmouth, June* 7, 1775 (Colden MS, New York Historical Society Library).

by which I was governed at that time I have experienced
on feveral trying occafions and never failed terminating
fucceffully   It is an Enthewfifm with which Soldiers cannot be too much Infpired when entering into action ; Indeed more or lefs of this Enthewfifm fhould govern every
ftep of a Soldier defirous of atchieving fame.   The fenti-
ment common in an army that he is a good Soldier who
does what he is ordered will feldom procure that fame
which ought to be the foldiers Glory.   To arrive at this
Goal it is neceffary not only to obey orders but to feek occafions of performing Enterprifes by voluntary fervices and
by projecting plans for anoying the Enemy—The meafure
directed by the Committee (who were vefted with the Government of the city) to fuffer the Britifh troops to depart
unmolefted with their arms and acoutraments tho no doubt
a proper one was not univerfally approved of, and as foon
as it was announced that the troops were on their march
and were taking with them feveral Carts loaded with fpare
arms a fudden determination of a few perfons who were
then affemblyd at a Mr Jefper Darkes who keept a public
houfe in Water Street near Beekman flip were the moft
zealous partizans in the caufe of Liberty ufed to have
dayly and nightly meetings.   It was about 12 oClock M.
when the account of this movement of the troops was
brought to Mr Drakes at which place I happened to be
at the time, and with the others then at that houfe fet out
to alarm the citizens in order to Collect force to prevent

the troops from carrying thofe fpare arms with them.   The
way I took and the difpatch I made brought me to the
front of the troops as they were marching, before any of
the other perfons who fet out on the fame bufinefs; On
my arrival in their front which was at the Corner of Beaver
ftreet in Broad ftreet I ftoped the horfe that was drawing
the front Cart-load of arms.   This of courfe occafioned a
halt in the Troops.   And brought the Major of the regiment[1] who was the comanding officer in front to enquire
into the caufe of the halt.   I had the horfe by the head
and on the appearance of the Major informed him that the
halt was made to prevent the fpare arms from being carried
off, as the act of the Committe did not authorife the troops
taking any other arms than fuch as they carried on their
backs,   while I was making this explanation to the Major
David Mathews Efquire who was at that time Mayor of
the city[2] came up And accofted me in the following words
I am furprifed Mr Willett that you will hazard the peace
and endanger the lives of our citizens when you know that
the Committee have directed that the troops fhall be permitted to depart unmolefted,   as Mr Mathews was a Tory
and zealous fupporter of the meafures of the Britifh Goverment His prefence or opinion could have no Influence

---

[1] Major Hamilton was appointed lieutenant in this regiment, October 1,
1755; captain, March 4, 1760; and major, December 16, 1764.   He
came to America with it in the latter year, and left the army in July, 1775.
—Army Lifs.

[2] Vide note 1, page 59.

with me, and I very unhefitatingly affured him that his furprife was not to furprife me that the Committee had not
authorifed the carrying off any fpare arms. That confidering the Bloody bufinefs which had taken place among our
Bretheren in Maffechufettes whom we were bound by the ties
of honor as well as Intereft to fupport, I deemed it my duty
to prevent thofe arms from being ufed againft them and
conceived that it would be much more reputable for us
to employ them in the defence of our Injured Country.
While this queftion was agitating with the Major and the
Mayor, Mr Governeer Morris[1] made his appearance, And
to my great aftonifhment Joined the Mayor in opinion.
Mr Morris's fituation was very different from that of the
Mayors, He was a Whig of very refpectable Connections
and tho young of Brilliant talents—To be oppofed by Mr.
Morris ftagard me—And I doubt whether all my Zeal
and Enthufaifm would fupported me had it not been for
the arrival at that Critical moment of John Morine Scott[2]

[1] Gouverneur Morris was born at Morrifania, N. Y., January 31, 1752,
and graduated at King's College, in New York, in 1768. He ftudied law
with William Smith; in May, 1775, was chofen a member of the Provincial Congrefs; and in October, 1777, a member of the Continental Congrefs. He reprefented Pennfylvania in the Convention which framed the
Federal Conftitution; in 1792, was appointed a minifter plenipotentiary to
France, where he remained until October, 1794; and in 1800, was chofen
a fenator from New York in the federal councils. He was one of the earlieft and moft ardent of the friends of the canal fyftem of New York; and
November 6, 1816, he died full of years and of honors.

[2] John Morin Scott, one of the earlieft, moft able, and moft determined
of "the Sons of Liberty" in New York, was born in that city in 1730, and

who was an Influencial member of the Committee and
whose reputation for talents was as great as any in the
city: He came up Juft as I was repeating to Mr. Morris
the reafons of my conduct And Exclaimed in a Loud voice
you are right Willett the committee have not given them
permiffion to carry off any fpare arms.   By this time the
throng of people around us had greatly Increafed and were
prefing in on every fide.   Mr. Scott's opinion was fcarcely
proclaimed when I turned the front Cart to the right and
directed the Cartman to drive up Beaver Street.   the other
Carts which were Loaded with arms were made to follow
and on the fuggeftion of Mr Scott that it would be proper
to addrefs the troops   I Jumped on a Cart, and after ob-
ferving to them that if it was their defire to Join the Bloody
bufinefs which was tranfacting near Bofton, we were ready
to meet them in the Sanguin field, But that if any of them
felt a repugnance to the unatural work of fheding the blood
of their Countrymen and would recover their arms and
march forward they fhould be protected   One of the fol-

graduated at Yale College in 1746. He adopted the profeffion of the law,
and foon became one of the leading members of the provincial bar, where
many of the ableft minds of America were then practifing. He was one of
the earlieft opponents of the government, and in 1775 he was a member of
the Provincial Congrefs; on the 9th of June, 1776, he was appointed brigadier
general of the provincial troops, with whom he was engaged in the battle of
Long Ifland; and in March, 1777, he left the fervice to become fecretary
of ftate of New York. In 1782 and 1783 he ferved in the Continental
Congrefs; and on the 14th of September, 1784, he died in the city of New
York.—Loffing's " *Field Book*," *II.*, p. 805.

ʼdiers recovering his arms and marching forward was received by three hearty Huzzas and together with the Carts
five in number loaded with Chests of arms Conducted with
the continual Huzzas of the Citizens through Beaver Street
& up the Broad Way as far as the Corner of John Street
where their was a Ball alley and Large Yard belonirg to
Mr Abraham Van Dyck who was a good Whig a pleafant faracious agreeable man—and who afterwards when the
British troops took poffeition of New York was made a prifoner and fuffered a long & Cruel Captavity—In this yard the
arms were depofited. Thefe arms and thofe taken poffeffion of on the arrival of the account of the Battle of Lexington were employed by the firft troops raifed in New
York under the orders of Congrefs.[1] The troops receiving
no other Impediment agreeable to the act of the Committee
Marched to the Wharf and embarked. Altho I have no
difpofition to Cenfer the act of the Committee Yet I was
then and am ftill of opinion that it would have been as eafy
to have made prifoners of the whole of the troops as it was
to take from them thefe fpare arms. But the Idea of a
Compromife with the British Goverment pervaded our councils, and checked the adoption of fpirited meafures.

[1] The firft regiment of "the New York line" was that of which Alexander McDougal was colonel; Rudolphus Ritzema, lieutenant colonel; and
Frederick Weiffenfels, major.

9

THE HICKEY PLOT.

I. LETTER FROM PETER T. CURTENIUS TO RICHARD VARICK.

[This letter was written by Peter T. Curtenius, the commiffary general of the New York line, to Colonel Richard Varick, and relates to the fo-called "HICKEY PLOT." That confpiracy, which had been organized by Governor Tryon from his retreat on " *The Duchefs of Gordon,*" aimed at a delivery of the city and the army to the royal forces; and its difcovery was productive of the moft intenfe excitement. The moft exaggerated ac-counts were fpread throughout the country, fuch as this letter muft have produced wherever it was read; and the Provincial Congrefs of New York, by a committee which it had previoufly appointed "for the hearing and try-ing difaffected perfons and thofe of equivocal characters," inveftigated the fubject in its minutiæ.

As is cuftomary in fuch cafes, efpecially when the parties employed have been taken, as was the cafe in this plot, from the beer-houfes and "low places" of the country, the leaders efcaped the juft penalty of their crimes by becoming witneffes againft their comrades; and of all the confpirators, one only, an Irifhman named THOMAS HICKEY, a private in the ranks of General Wafhington's body guard, was capitally punifhed.

Interefting accounts of the plot may be found in Gordon's "American Revolution" (ed. London, 1788,) II., pp. 276, 277; Marfhall's "Wafhing-ton," II., p. 392; Irving's "Wafhington," II., pp. 242–246; "Proceedings of the Committee for the Hearing," etc., June 22-26, 1776; "Minutes of the General Court Martial which tried Thomas Hickey," etc.]

N YORK June 22d 1776—

SR

Inclofed is Capt Staat's Rect for a tent &c which pleafe to Endorfe on the back that you have received it. Your father is well who was at my houfe yefterday. Your good mother & the rest of the family are also in good health, having seen them a few days ago at Hackinsack.

Last night was discovered a most Infernal plott against the lives of Gen[1] Washington & Putnem &c—Some of the Villains concerned are in safe custody   among them are Mr Matthews our Mayor[1] Gilbert Forbes a Gunsmith,[2]

[1] David Matthews was appointed Mayor upon the resignation of Whitehead Hicks, in February, 1776, and was among those who were implicated in the intricacies of the Hickey plot.   There is nothing in the evidence, however, which justifies the suspicion that he was really concerned in it, beyond acting as a messenger in delivering money to Forbes from Tryon.   He was removed into Connecticut, and held in close custody there for some time; but he was subsequently released, and held the office of Registrar in Admiralty, in 1782, under the British authorities.

[2] Gilbert Forbes was a gunsmith doing business opposite to Hull's Tavern, No. 18 Broadway.   It has been said by some that he was an Irishman; but his father, who died in 1769, had been a resident of New York for many years, and had done a large business as a hardware merchant.

Gilbert appears to have been an early participant in the plot, if not one of the originators of the scheme; and through his hands the money, which had been provided by the enemy, passed into those of the recruits.   The latter appear also to have taken the oath of allegiance before him; and to some extent, at least, he appears to have directed the proposed operations of the conspirators.

When the plot had been discovered, he was arrested and thrown into irons, steadily refusing to divulge the secrets which he possessed; but a short time afterward, when Mr. Livingston visited him under the pretence of sympathizing with him in view of his approaching execution, he begged permission to go before the Congress and to divulge all he knew about the matter. His proposition appears to have been accepted; and his testimony will be found in the report of the trial of Hickey by a general court martial, on the 26th of June, as well as before a committee of the Provincial Congress of New York on the 29th of the same month; and he appears to have escaped punishment probably through this means.

He is described as " a short thick man, with a white coat."

a fifer & Drum^r of Genl Wafhingtons Guard^1 &c   the particulars are not yet Tranfpiered, the culprits are to be ex-
amin^d before congrefs this day^2 thus much is tranfpiered
(from officers who were employed to apprehend them),
that a great fum was offered to affaffinate Gen^ls Wafhington & Putnam^3, that a plan was found in their poffeffion of
all the fortifications,^{4} That whilft the Regulars made the attack fome perfons were to blow up the powder houfe^5 &
others were to deftroy Kings brige to prevent reenforce-
ments coming in from New England^6 In fhort the plott

^{1} The *drummer* was " William Green," who appears to have been very
active, adminiftering the oath of allegiance to the lefs fortunate Hickey, and
receiving a brokerage of " one dollar per man from Forbes for every man
he fhall inlift."   As he was the leading witnefs againft Hickey, when the
latter was tried before the court martial, there is no doubt that he efcaped
the punifhment which was fo juftly his due.

The fifer was James Johnfon, but he does not appear to have taken any
active part in the confpiracy.

^{2} The prifoners were examined by a committee of the Provincial Congrefs of New York : Philip Livingfton, John Jay, Gouverneur Morris, Jofeph
Hallett, Thomas Tredwell, Lewis Graham, and Leonard Ganfevoort, con-
ftituting the committee.

^{3} There does not appear in evidence any fuch purpofe on the part of the
confpirators, although rumors of the day were numerous and decided.

^{4} There is no evidence of fuch "a plan" having been found on any perfon ; nor is there much reafon to believe that fuch a plan exifted, or was
neceffary, where all concerned were refidents of the city, or had been within a
fhort time, and knew all the localities which would have appeared on fuch a plan.

^{5} " The powder houfe" in queftion ftood on the fouth-weftern bank of
" *The Frefh-water,*" near the prefent junction of Centre and Pearl ftreets.
There is no allufion to any propofed deftruction of the magazine in any part
of the evidence which was taken at that time.

^{6} The drummer, William Green, in his teftimony taken before the court

was a moſt damnable one & I hope that the Villains may
receive a puniſhment equal to perpetual Itching without
the benifit of ſcratching

I am Sᵣ your moſt

Obed Servₜ

PETER T. CURTENIUS.[1]

martial which tried Hickey, teſtified that "all that Forbes propoſed to me
was, that when the king's forces arrived, we *ſhould cut away King's Bridge*,
and then go on board a ſhip of war, which would be in the Eaſt River to
receive us." Gilbert Forbes, the gunſmith, when examined before the Provincial Congreſs, after narrating the plans of the conſpirators in their defigns
upon different parts of the iſland, teſtified, "that ſhould they gain poſſeſſion
of the places above-mentioned, their next objeſt would be the grounds ad-
jacent to King's Bridge, where they intend to erect ſtrong works, *ſo as to cut
off the communication between the city and country.*"

[1] Peter Theobaldus Curtenius was born in the city of New York in
1734, and was the ſon of the Rev. Anthonius Curtenius, a clergyman of the
Dutch Church, who came from Holland ſome years previous, and at the time
of his death, in October, 1756, was ſettled over a congregation in Kings
county. The genealogical tree of the family commences with Peter Curtenius, born 1390, at Zingoon, in the diſtrict named Curten, three miles from
Eberfield, and is continued down to 1734.

Peter T. Curtenius, before and at the time of the Revolution, was a merchant in the city of New York. In Auguſt, 1755, he married Miſs Catharine Goelet, the daughter of Phillipus Goelet of ſaid city. No higher
meed of praiſe can be beſtowed on him than to ſay that he was a true
friend of his country, and an ardent patriot in the days of the Revolution.
In 1774, he was an active member of the committee of correſpondence with
the ſiſter colonies, appointed by the citizens of New York,[1] and in May, 1775,
he was choſen on the general committee of the city and county. During the
war he held the office of Commiſſary General, with the rank of colonel under
the Provincial Congreſs, as appears by numerous letters as ſuch with the com-

(1) See *American Colonial Archives*, 4th ſeries, vol. 1, pages 293 to 330, as to the
committee and proceedings.

II. JOHN VARICK, JR., TO CAPT. RICHARD VARICK, SECRETARY TO GENERAL SCHUYLER AT ALBANY.

NEW YORK June 25th 1776   Tuefday

Dear Brother

Since my laft, Matters here, have taken a new Turn; for one fourth of the Citizens have been oblidg'd

mittee and Congrefs, found in the "American Colonial Archives"[1] and "The Colonial Documents" publifhed by the ftate of New York, from which it appears that to fupply the wants of the army, he was compelled to make large advances from his own means and on his own credit. At one time, when the refources and credit of Congrefs had entirely failed, and a fupply of clothing and fhoes for a deftitute army was abfolutely required, Colonel Curtenius converted his own houfe and ftore on the corner of Liberty ftreet and Broadway, into money, and expended the amount of fixteen hundred pounds towards purchafing thefe neceffary fupplies for its relief; which, at the clofe of the war, was refunded to him by the general government, in Continental money of no value. It is related of him that he was unwilling to wear any article of foreign manufacture, and that his wedding-fuit was of domeftic ftuff. In 1792, the legiflature created the office of ftate auditor, and Colonel Curtenius was appointed to the office, and continued to hold it until 1797, when the office of comptroller was created in its place.

He died in the city of New York, of the yellow fever, in 1798, and was buried in the vault at the entrance of the Middle Dutch Church, on Cedar ftreet, where his remains refted until 1857, when, with the remains of his fon, General Peter Curtenius (who died in 1817), they were removed to Beechwood Cemetery in New Rochelle, and depofited with the remains of his daughter, Mrs. Jane Roofevelt, in the vault of her family.

He left him furviving, his wife, who lived until 1806, and his children—General Peter Curtenius, who was appointed United States marfhal by Jefferfon, in 1806, and continued to about the clofe of the war of 1812; Jane Roofevelt, the wife of Elbert Roofevelt, late of Pelham; Catharine Dunlap, the wife of the Rev. John Dunlap, late of Cambridge, Wafhington county,

(1) See "Archives," 4th feries, vol. 2, pages 1124 and 1337

to turn out, either as Volanteers, or by Draught, in Confequence of the Exprefs from the Continental Congrefs.¹ The firft Batalion is to have its Number compleated out of thofe that have been draughted & be commanded by Col: Lafher².—Eighteen of the Fufileer Company, turn'd out Volanteers and the remainder were draughted³.—I hap-

New York; and Mary and Elizabeth, unmarried; all of whom are alfo deceafed. There are none of the name now known in the United States, except his grandchildren, viz.: John L. Curtenius, of the city of Buffalo; Henry R. Curtenius and Frederick W. Curtenius, of Kalamazoo, Michigan, and their children, and thofe of Alfred G. Curtenius, late of Peoria, Illinois, deceafed.

On the 9th day of July, 1776, the equeftrian ftatue of King George the III., placed on a pedeftal in the Bowling Green in New York city, was, by the Sons of Freedom, proftrated to the duft, and out of its materials 42,083 cartridges were fupplied with balls, and thus returned to the loyal fubjects of his majefty. The pedeftal remained until after 1820. In this tranfaction Colonel Curtenius is ftated to have been one of the leading fpirits.

¹ "All the male inhabitants between fixteen and fixty years of age, were fubject" to thefe drafts.—*Cafe of William Butler, Aff. Com. Gen. (Tomlinfon MSS.)*

² This regiment was compofed of the "Independent Foot Companies" then exifting in this city. They were the Grenadier Company, the Fuziliers, the German Fuziliers, the Union Company, the Sportfman Company, the Corficans, the Bold Forrefters, the Light Infantry, the Ofwago Rangers, two companies of Artillery, and a company of Rangers. The uniforms of the companies were different—no two companies appear to have worn the fame uniform; and the officers embraced the moft refpectable citizens, many of them members of the "Sons of Liberty." Among the line officers were Abraham Brafher, Rudolphus Ritzema, Samuel Broome, William Malcolm, Nicholas Roofevelt, Frederic Jay, Frederic De Peyfter, Marinus Willet, Jeremiah Wool, and Nicholas Bogart.

³ "*The Fufileer Company*" here fpoken of was Captain Ritzema's company, of which Henry G. Livingfton, Andrew Lott, and James Van Zandt, were lieutenants. Its uniform was blue, with red facings. The cap was

pen'd to be included amongſt the Draughts; for the Engagement I am under to the Doctor¹, & the Care of the
Houſe will hardly admit Me, to be a Soldier, 'tho it has
fallen to my Lott, much leſs to turn out as Volanteer.   I
am almoſt determin'd to get a Man in my Place, till ſuch
Times, as I may with Honor & Juſtice to Myſelf be ab-
ſolv'd from that Engagement; and then I will with all
imaginable Pleaſure repair to my Company again, and un-

of bear ſkin.   On the cap and pouch were braſs plates, bearing the
word, "Fuziliers," and encircling the laſt, "*Salus populi ſuprema lex
eſt.*"

¹ "*The Doctor.*"   This refers to Dr. Middleton, with whom Mr. Varick
and others were purſuing their medical ſtudies.   On the 26th of April, Dr.
Middleton, from prudential motives—he being a Tory, as will be ſeen from
this letter—ſuddenly failed for Bermuda, " in company with Ld. Drummond,
John McAdam, and Harry Nicolls," leaving his houſe, library, inſtruments,
and bills receivable in the hands of Mr. Varick and his fellow-ſtudent,
Charles Mitchell, while his family removed to Fluſhing, Long Iſland.   Speak-
ing of the privileges thus afforded him, Mr. Varick, in a previous letter, ſays,
"now that we had Peace, I'd engage that I would make ſuch uſe of my Time,
as would be of infinite Service to Me.   But Oh the Times, the Times, have
ſuch an Effect on Me, that all my Reading and Studying prove of little Advantage."

Peter Middleton, M. D., was a native of Scotland, and a graduate of
the Univerſity of Edinburgh.   He came to New York in 1752, and very
ſoon after occupied a high rank in his profeſſion.   In 1767, he was appointed
Profeſſor of the Theory of Phyſic in King's College.   He was the phyſician
of Governor Tryon, and by permiſſion of the Provincial Congreſs of New
York, he was on the 13th of February, 1776, permitted to viſit his excellency on board the ſhip "Ducheſs of Gordon."   On the 21ſt of February,
he was allowed to continue his profeſſional viſits "untill the further order of
this Congreſs."   He publiſhed ſeveral important papers on medical ſubjects,
and died in the city of New York, in January, 1781, of ſchirrus of the
ſtomach.

dergo with becoming Affignation, & Willingnefs, in Con-
junction with my fellow Soldiers; whatever Duty and Hard-
fhip may be affign'd for them. But now the Confideration
of the Pledge I made of my Honor & Fidelity to the
Doctor, is of fo great Moment to me, that it renders Part of
my Life uncomfortable, leaft I fhould be in any one Point
deficient in the Difcharge of my Duty.

Laft Friday I had the Pleafure of receiving a Letter from
the Doct'. dated Bermuda May 13th. He makes mention
that he intended to return in a few Weeks, but I am in-
clin'd to think that He'll avoid coming to this City, if he
hears how the Tories have been treated here, till Matters
are in Some Meafure come to a Determination. From
what he writes & from the Things he has left behind
Him I have great reafon to conclude that he really intended to return at the Time limited, notwithftanding the Inti-
mations of thofe who pretended to know to the contrary,
for I was fatiffy'd that it was inconfiftent with that Frank-
nefs which the Doctor is diftinguifh'd by, that he fhould be
guilty of fuch Deceit towards Us. When to expect Him
I am at a Lofs, but I am determin'd to fend his medical
Books and Surgical Inftruments to Hackinfack, that if I
fhould, in fhort get clear of the Army, and the Doct'. not return, I may have them at my Command, & the Perufal of
them.

Gov' Trion[1] has given evident Proofs how he intends to

___

[1] William Tryon was commiffioned captain in the Firft Foot Guards, Oct.

10

fight againft Us (altho' he pledged every Thing that is honorable to the contrary) by engaging Gill: Forbes with large Sums of Money, to procure Rifle Guns & Mufquets for Him[1]; & likewife engaging Forbes in a Plot to affaf- finate and maffacre his fellow Citizens[2]; But how happily it was difcover'd. This is the Rafcal in whom all Confi- dence was put, & in whom the utmoft Fidelity was re- pofed; that he would procure Peace & be the Means of reinftating this Province in a ftate of perfect Happinefs, if it could by any Means be accomplifh'd. How has he abufed that Confidence? which has perverted all the Love & Re- fpect he once enjoy'd amongft the Inhabitants of this Prov- ince, in the moft infuperable Hatred. Laft Saturday after- noon, by order of Congrefs, a Detachment of 14 Men

12, 1751. In October, 1764, he was appointed lieutenant governor of North Carolina, and fucceeded Governor Dobbs as governor in July, 1765. In July, 1771, he was tranfferred to the government of New York, where his career was productive of no honor to himfelf or benefit to the colony. On the 25th May, 1772, he was appointed colonel in the army; on the 8th June, 1775, third major in the Guards; on the 29th Auguft, 1777, major general of the army; and on the 14th May, 1778, colonel of the 70th regi- ment of the line. Having refigned the nominal office of governor of New York, on the 21ft March, 1780, and returned to England, he was appointed lieutenant general of the army, November 20, 1782, and colonel of the 29th regiment, on the 16th Auguft, 1783. He died in London, January 27th, 1788.

[1] Governor Tryon had employed Forbes to make a number of rifles and mufkets; and the payment for them was made through David Matthews, mayor of the city, as appeared from the teftimony which was offered on the trial of Thomas Hickey.

[2] *Vide* Note 3, page 68.

(amongſt whom I was included) under Capt W^m. Livingſton was ſent over to Long-Iſland, in Purſuit of one who was ac-cuſed of being concern'd in this curſed Plot. We rid all Sat-urday Night, & Sunday Morning half after three we arrived at the Place we were order'd for; But could not find the Man; in our return we met one on the road who anſwer'd in every Reſpect the Diſcripſion given of Him, which made Us conclude that he muſt be the Perſon we were in Queſt of. We return'd ſafe on Sunday Evening being much fatigued, having had no Sleep while out. Inquiry being made, the Man was found innocent and acquited. This is the firſt Expedition any part of the Batalion has been on ſince they have become Provincial Soldiers; and I think the Fuſileers deſerve the Honor of initiating Such Expeditions.

Capt. Wm. Livingſton was yeſterday choſen by a Majority of Votes of the officers of the firſt Batalion as Major. in Preference to Capt. Jno. Rooſevelt', who has been a nominal one ſince the Batalion has been in Pay. Wm. Wilcocks ſucceeds Wm Livingſton as Capt. & Ralph Thurman who was a few Days ſince a Private, ſteps in as Firſt Lieut. What large ſtrides ſome of the Privates in the Fuſileer Coompy have already taken to Popularity.

from Yours moſt affectionately

JOHN VARICK JUN^R

Capt. R^d. Varick² Albany

Captain John Rooſevelt was captain of the Oſwago Rangers.

² Captain Richard Varick was born in 1752, and was educated for the bar. When the colonial troubles broke out, he tendered his ſervices to General

III. LETTER FROM SOLOMON DROWNE[1], M. D., TO MISS SALLY DROWNE, OF PROVIDENCE, R. I.

Dear Sister

* * * * *

A most infernal Plot has lately been discovered here, which, had it been put in Execution, wou'd have made

Schuyler, and was appointed military secretary of that officer. He remained in that department after the removal of General Schuyler from that command, until after the surrender of General Burgoyne, in 1777; when he was appointed inspector general of the troops in the Highlands. After the defection of General Arnold, Colonel Varick entered the military family of General Washington, where he remained until the close of the war.

On the restoration of peace, he became recorder of New York; in 1789, he was appointed attorney general of the state; and, in the same year, mayor of New York, which latter office he held during twelve years.

He was president of the Society of the Cincinnati during upwards of thirty years; and, on the decease of Mr. Boudinot, he was elected president of the American Bible Society.

He died at Jersey City, July 30, 1831.

[1] Solomon Drowne, M. D., was born in Providence, Rhode Island, March 11th, 1753. His father, Solomon Drowne, senior, was a merchant of Providence, and for more than half a century one of its prominent citizens. At the age of twenty, the son graduated at Brown University, and soon after commenced the study of medicine at the University of Pennsylvania.

Dr. Drowne served for several years as surgeon in the Revolutionary Army. From his letters written at that period, it appears that he arrived in New York, June 3d, 1776; called the next day upon Dr. John Morgan, director general of the hospitals; and on the day following (the 5th) entered the service of the United States, as surgeon's mate in the general hospital. He was in this city at the time of its evacuation by the American troops, and remained at the hospital among the last, packing up the medicines, until the British were so near, that the boat in which he embarked up the North River

America tremble; and been as fatal a ftroke to us (*this
country,*) as Gun-Powder Treafon wou'd to England, had
it fucceeded. The Hellifh Confpirators were a Number of
Tories (the Mayor of yᵉ City among them) and three of
Genˡ Wafhington's Life-Guards. The Plan was to kill
Generals Wafhington and Putnam, and as many other
commanding officers as poffible.—I fhou'd have mentioned

was only about two gun-fhots ahead of them. He was ftationed at Weftchefter, North Caftle, and other places in the ftate of New York, and at Nor-
walk, in Connecticut. His letters to his family in Providence, while in the
public fervice, breathe the pureft patriotic ardor; and though they occafion-
ally allude to privations and the fad fcenes of hofpital life, they at the fame
time evince that his duty to his country was invariably uppermoft in his heart.
In fact, whilft engaged in his profeffional ftudies before coming to New York,
he took an active intereft in the military affairs of his native city, Providence,
preparing, as it was, for the revolutionary ftruggle; and affifted, himfelf, in
throwing up the fortifications in that vicinity. In 1777, he was in the Rhode
Ifland State Hofpital for feven months; ftill later, he was furgeon for a fimilar period to Colonel Crary's regiment; and in Auguft, 1778, was in Sullivan's expedition againft Rhode Ifland, where he alfo performed active fervice.
After this, he was ftationed for a time at Briftol, Rhode Ifland; and on the
3d of Auguft, 1780, he was appointed furgeon to Lieutenant Colonel Atwell's
regiment.

At the conclufion of the war, Dr. Drowne entered upon the practice of
his profeffion in Providence. In 1784, he vifited the hofpitals and medical
fchools of London and Paris, for the purpofe of profecuting ftill further his
medical ftudies. Shortly after his return he journeyed to Ohio, and refided
for nearly a year at Marietta, where, on the 13th of January, 1789, he delivered a funeral addrefs on General Varnum; and on April 7th of the fame
year, an oration in commemoration of the fettlement of that place by the
Ohio Company. Subfequently he refumed his practice at Providence; but
in confequence of ill-health, removed again to the Weft in 1792, and fettled
for a time at Morgantown, Va.; and after the border incurfions of the Indians were over, he proceeded to Union, Penn. Here he delivered a funera,

at firft,—to fet the City on fire in nine feveral Places.—To fpike up the Cannon: Then to give a Signal to the Afia and Ships expected;—and blow up the magazine.   They had a large Body of Men, which were to attack ours amidft their Confufion.   The whole was difcovered (as I am informed) by a fergt of ye Guards, whom they wanted to take into the Plot, and who, having got what he cou'd from them, difcovered all to the General.   The Drummer of ye Guards was to have ftabb'd ye General.   The pretty

addrefs on General Wafhington, "in conformity to the Proclamation of the Prefident of the United States," February 22, 1800.   In 1801, he retraced his fteps to Rhode Ifland, and fettled in the town of Fofter, where he paffed the remainder of his days engaged in profeffional and agricultural purfuits, and in the cultivation of his tafte for botany and elegant letters.   In 1811, he was appointed profeffor of Materia Medica and Botany in Brown Univerfity, and gave courfes of lectures in that inftitution for many years.   The Rhode Ifland Medical Society (of which Dr. Drowne was fubfequently vice-prefident), in 1819, chofe him a delegate to the convention which formed the National Pharmacopœia.   At the requeft of the citizens of Providence, on February 23d, 1824, he delivered an "oration in aid of the caufe of the Greeks," whofe unequal ftruggle with the Turks was at that time calling forth the fympathy and affiftance of this country.   During the fame year, he publifhed a "Compendium of Agriculture, or the Farmer's Guide in the moft effential parts of Hufbandry and Gardening;" and on feveral occafions he delivered the annual addreffes before the State Agricultural Society, in the organization and proceedings of which he bore an active part.

Dr. Drowne was diftinguifhed not only in his profeffion but as a lecturer and writer on botany, of which fcience he was an enamored votary from early youth; and his occafional orations, addreffes, and literary and fcientific papers, a large number of which have been publifhed, won for him a high reputation as a finifhed and erudite fcholar.   He died February 5th, 1834.

The prefent efficient Secretary of the National Fire Infurance Company of the city of New York (Henry T. Drowne) is his grandfon.

Fellows are in fafe Cuftody, and I hope I fhall be able to give you a better account of them in my next. This Morning a large Guard went to take two hundred Tories who are under Arms not very far from this City.   *   *

Yours,

SOLOMON DROWNE.

IV. LETTER FROM SOLOMON DROWNE, M. D., TO WILLIAM DROWNE[1], ESQ., PROVIDENCE.

GENERAL HOSPITAL, N. YORK July 13th 1776.

Dear Billy,

    *   *   *   *   *   *

It is now almoft Midnight, and but a little while fince I returned to my Chamber from carrying Medicine to one of

[1] William Drowne, born in Providence, Rhode Ifland, April 17th, 1755, was the brother of Dr. Solomon Drowne. From early youth, he took an active interest in the military affairs of Rhode Ifland and Maffachufetts; and was engaged in the fervice of his country during the Revolutionary War, in a variety of offices. On June 2d, 1775, he became an officer in the Mendon regiment (Colonel Read's), which was ftationed at Roxbury, Maffachufetts, and continued with the regiment until the clofe of the year. In January, 1776, his name heads the lift of lieutenants of the Rhode Ifland Brigade. A year later he was adjutant of Colonel Bowen's regiment at Pawtuxet, Rhode Ifland; and in 1778, ferved as quartermafter general, with the rank of captain.

Mr. Drowne poffeffed an adventurous fpirit, which led him at a later period to embark, on feveral occafions, in the private floops-of-war that were fitted out from New England ports; and which often bravely contended with the enemy's armed veffels, thereby rendering efficient fervice to the United States. In his cruifes in the privateer fhip "General Wafhington," of Providence, and the "Belifarius" of Bofton, he kept private journals, in

yᵉ Wards I have yᵉ Care of, and applying a Poultice to a
Man's foot, over which a Gun Carriage run Yefterday, in
the Battle with yᵉ Ships; for a further account of which
fee Sally's Letter:—So you may judge how much time I
have to write. *   ⁂   *   ⁂   ⁂

I heartily congratulate you, my dear Brother, on being
an Inhabitant of yᵉ Free an Independant States of America. I herewith fend you a Gazette which contains yᵉ Declaration; and alfo an Extract of a Letter from Philadelphia, which, if you have not had yet, fhou'd be glad you
wou'd fhow Tommy Ruffell.

The Declaration was read, agreeable to general Orders,
at yᵉ Head of yᵉ Brigade, &c. this week; and loud Huzzas expreff'd the approbation of yᵉ Freeborn Bands.

The Night following, the famous gilded equeftrian ftatue
of yᵉ Britifh King, in this City, was levelled with yᵉ Duft:
his head taken off, and next morning, in a Wheel-Barrow
carried to his Excellency's Quarters, I was told. There is
a large Quantity of Lead about it, which is to be run into
Bullets to deftroy his Myrmidons. I fuppofe you have

which were noted down many occurrences of hiftorical intereft. While on
board the Belifarius, during the fummer of 1781, he was taken prifoner, carried to New York, and confined for three months in the foul and reeking
hold of the Old Jerfey prifon fhip. Here his health fuffered extremely, until
in November of that year he was permitted to be abfent awhile at Newport,
on parole. But the feeds of difeafe had become too deeply rooted in his
previoufly robuft conftitution by this fevere imprifonment, ever to be erad-
icated. He rallied from a painful illnefs only to linger along, with enfeebled
health, until Auguft, 1786, when he died. He was buried at Providence.

heard of ye Execution of one of the General's Guards, concerned in ye hellish Plot, difcovered here fome time paft.
There was a vaft Concourfe of People to fee ye poor Fellow
hanged.

14th I heard this Evening, that Lord How had fent a F ag
with a Letter directed to *George Waſhington Efq*, and that it
was returned unopened becaufe he gave him not his proper
title;—tho' ye Capt^r that brought it faid its Contents were of
the utmoft Importance, and that Ld How was very forry
he had not arrived a few Days fooner (Perhaps before Independence was declared, for 'tis faid he is invefted with
unlimited Power.)   This may learn him a little Manners.
Well; two Ships & 3 tenders up N. River;—Communication with Canada by water cut off:—Something important
will turn up foon

    *   *   *   *   *

I am very tired, and it is paft Midnight.

    Write often to your Friend & Brother

                    SOLOMON DROWNE

11

[No form of record retains fo much of frefhnefs and lafting intereft as that contained in private correfpondence. Coming from the very times and the very fpot which we are confidering, it embodies the fpirit of the hour with a fidelity which the more pains-taking and correct hiftorian labors in vain to feize. The letters from which the following extracts are taken, were written in New York city at that anxious period which, following clofe upon the events of Lexington and Bunker Hill, preceded the battle of Long Ifland and the confequent evacuation, in September, 1776, of New York city by the American forces, who were no more to enter it until its final Evacuation by the Britifh in November, 1783.]

GILBERT LIVINGSTON TO DR. PETER TAPPAN.

New York July 29th 1775.[1]

Dear Brother

You will fee by the Warrants who are nominated officers for your County[2], it is very likely we fhall raife an additional number of Troops befides the 3000 now Raized We Expect all diligence will be ufed in Recruiting, that the Regiments may be formed immediately

Laft Sunday about Two oclock the Generals Wafhington Lee & Schuyler arrived here[3] they Croffed the North

---

[1] By referring to General Wafhington's letter to "the members of the Continental Congrefs, Philadelphia," dated "New York, 25 *June*, 1775," it will be feen that this date is *incorrect*.

[2] Dr. Tappan belonging to Poughkeepfie, in Dutchefs county, this remark muft refer to that county.

[3] The fubject of the reception of General Wafhington at New York, while on his way to Bofton, was one of unufual intereft.

River at Hoback[1] & Landed at Coll Lifpenards[2] there were
8 or 10 Companies under Arms all in Uniforms who
Marched out to Lifpenards, the proceffion began from
there thus, the Companies firft, Congrefs next two of Continental Congrefs next General Officers next & a Company
of Horfe from philadelphia Who Came with the General
brought up the Rear[3] there were an innumerable Company
of people Men Women & Children prefent

in the evening Governor Tryon[4] landed as in the news
paper[5] I walked with my Friend George Clinton[6] all the
way to Lifpenards—Who is now gone home

General Schuyler had written from Newark, requefting the Provincial Congrefs to fend a delegation to meet the General; and Meffrs. Smith, Hobert,
Gouverneur Morris, and Rich'd Montgomery, were appointed for that purpofe.

The arrival of Governor Tryon at the fame time was a fource of embar-
raffment; and a curious and not very creditable fpectacle was prefented, the
particulars of which afford a fair picture of the "*trimming*" propenfities of
many of the parties then in power in this colony.

[1] Hoboken.

[2] Colonel Lifpenard's refidence, near which General Wafhington appears
to have landed, was in the vicinity of Laight ftreet, near Greenwich ftreet.

[3] The company of horfe here referred to, was "a Troop of Gentlemen
of the Philadelphia Light Horfe, commanded by Capt. Markoe." It continued the efcort to King's bridge, when it returned to the city, arriving
here on Tuefday and remaining until Thurfday, when it returned home.

[4] Governor William Tryon, who had arrived in the fhip *Juliana*, Captain Montgomery, from London, landed at eight o'clock in the evening of
the fame day (*Sunday*, *June* 25), and was efcorted by great numbers of
people to the refidence of the Hon. Hugh Wallace.

[5] Gaine, in his "*New York Gazette and Mercury*," does not allude to
either of the arrivals referred to; Rivington, in his "*Gazetteer*" of the 28th
June, gives an account of Tryon's reception.

[6] Subfequently Governor George Clinton.

I am Very Well hope all Friends fo, the Torys Catey[1] Writes are as Violent as ever,! poor Infignificant Souls, Who think themfelves of great importance The Times will foon fhew. I fancy that they muft quit their Wicked Tenets, at leaft in pretence and fhew fair, Let their Hearts be as Black as Hell. Go on, be fpirited, & I doubt not, Succefs will Crown our Honeft endeavours for the fupport of our Juft Rights and Privaledges

✳

JOHN MORIN SCOTT[2] TO COLONEL RICHARD VARICK.

GREENWICH[3] Nov 15, 1775.

✳

Every office fhut up almoft but Sam. Jones's who will work for 6/ a day & Live accordingly—All Bufinefs ftagnated the City half deferted for fear of a Bombardment —a new Congrefs elected—Thofe for New York you will fee by the papers are changed for the better—All ftaunch Whigs now—How it is with the Convention I know not We have [not rec^d] Returns—Yefterday the new Congrefs was to meet but I believe they did not

---

[1] "*Catey*," wife of Gilbert Livingfton, and fifter of the Dr. Tappan to whom this letter was written.

[2] Subfequently General John Morin Scott, for a biographical fketch of whom, fee note 2, page 63.

[3] He refided in the feat fince known as "*The Hermitage*" and "*The Temple of Health*," which remained, until a recent date, in Weft Fortythird ftreet, between the Eighth and Ninth avenues.

make a Houſe¹—my Doctors ſay I muſt not attend it nor any other Buſineſs in ſome Weeks; but I hope they will be miſtaken—Nothing from t'other ſide of the Water but a fearful looking for of Wrath—Our continental petition moſt probably contemned the Bulk of the nation (it is ſaid agᵗ Us) and a bloody Campaign next Summer—But let us be prepared for the worſt—Who can prize life without Liberty? It is a Bauble only fit to be thrown away.

✻   ✻   ✻   ✻   ✻

GARISH HARSIN TO MR. WILLIAM RADCLIFT AT RHYN BECK.

NEW YORK February 13, 1776

Couſen William

✻   ✻   ✻   ✻

i ſhall Now indever to Give you ſome acount how matters are hear Now on the 2 Inſtant arived Cornel Water Berry whit about 1000 men² the 3 Inſtant arived 500 minet men from New England a Number of pepol Began to move this Day out of town³ But on the 4 Inſtant in the morning arived General Clinton⁴ in the Mer-

¹ The new Provincial Congreſs was to have met on the 14th November ("Journal of the Provincial Congreſs of New York," p. 197), but a quorum was not preſent until December 6, 1775.

² "A regiment of Connecticut men, commanded by Colonel Waterbury."—Governor Tryon to the Earl of Dartmouth, 8th February, 1776.

³ Vide Butler's Statement (Tomlinſon MSS.), and Gov. Tryon's diſpatch to the Earl of Dartmouth, Feb. 8, 1776.

⁴ Sir Henry Clinton, who was then on his way to the South, to join Admiral Parker in his movement on South Carolina.

cury Man of Waar from Boſten & tranſport Brig the ſame
Day arived Generel Lee[1] Whit 300 men it is imboſ-
feble to Deſcrib the Convuſen[2] that this City was in on
acount of the Regelers Being Com[3] ſome ſaid ther was 15
fail Below & would Be up the Nex Day the 5 Inſten
Nothing materel Hapned pepel moving as fas as poſſeble
they could the 6 Inſten the River full of iſe the manawar
had her Cable cut by it but Let Go a Nother Ancker[4] the
7 Inſtant Lord Sterling[5] arived whit 1000 men from the

---

[1] General Waſhington, having obtained intelligence of the fitting out of a
fleet at Boſton, and of the embarkation of troops from there * * gave
orders to General Lee to repair, with ſuch volunteers as were willing to join
him and could be expeditiouſly raiſed, to the city of New York, with a de-
ſign to prevent the Engliſh from taking poſſeſſion of New York and the North
River, as they would thereby command the country and the communication
with Canada.—*Memoirs of Charles Lee, Eſq.* (London, 1792), pp. 12, 13.

[2] " *Convuſen*"—confuſion.

[3] " This City is in Terror and confuſion : One half of its inhabitants have
withdrawn with their effects, hundreds without means to ſupport their families."—*Governor Tryon to Earl of Dartmouth, 8th February*, 1776.

[4] " The Aſia and Phœnix have been obliged to draw very near the Wharfs,
having been much diſtreſſed by the floating cakes of ice."—*Governor Tryon
to Earl of Dartmouth, February* 8, 1776.

[5] William Alexander, Earl of Stirling, was born in the city of New York,
in 1726; ſucceeded his father as ſurveyor general of New Jerſey; and entered into trade. He accompanied General Shirley as his aide and ſecretary;
with whom he alſo viſited Europe in 1756–7. He was appointed a brigadier
general in the Continental Army, on the firſt of March, 1776—having pre-
viouſly commanded the Firſt regiment of the New Jerſey line.

He was captured at the battle of Long Iſland ; was ſubſequently in
command in New Jerſey, where he rendered effective ſervice ; was engaged at the Short Hills, Middlebrook, Brandywine, Germantown, and
Monmouth ; and during the entire war was actively engaged, doing good

jerfeys' the 8 Inftant added New Life to the moving for about 3 oclock arived a fhip Whit 200 Soulders from Bof-ton it is impoffeble to Defcrib the Confternation the Weoman Where in as a Report pravail that 19 fhip where Below however ther was no moor the 9 & 10 Inftant Nothing materel hapned pepol moeving as if it was the Laft Day as Gennerel Lee was to Begin to intrenfh the 12 Inftant the 11 Inftant was a Remarkable Day Gards Being plas all along the Eaft River fo as to prevent any perfons Going of the Begun to taik the Guns of they Batrey wich was Conducted whit fo much fecretfey that the fhip Did Not hear of it till 4 clock in the after Noon When they Imedetly hauld of in the River where they are Now whitout firing one Gun the Same Day failed the Mercury Manawar whit Generel Clinton on Board & the 2 tranfport for the wefward as it is faid we are Now under No fear from the fhip Now as we have men & guns fuffifent for them Now 12 Inftant pepol now Begin to ftop mov-ing our famely are all in York yet But fhall fend them to Brunfwick if we fe any Danger

N. B. We are Now a City of Waar

fervice for his country. He died at Albany, January 15, 1783, aged fifty-feven years.

Judge Duer of this city, recently deceafed, was his grandfon.

[1] "The day before yefterday Lord Sterling, at the head of four companies of Jerfey troops arrived here, and more are expected."—*Governor Tryon to Earl of Dartmouth, 8th Feb., 1776.*

ABRAHAM VARICK TO CAPT. RICHARD VARICK.

NEW YORK March 28th 1776.

Dear Brother

　　※　　　　　　※　　　　　　※　　　　※

I give you & every friend to Liberty Joy on the Regulars being drove from the Town of Bofton[1], it was a Neft they ought to have been from fome time ago, but all for the better perhaps, they would have ketcht us unprepar'd then, but now we are and will be fo well fortifyed, as to give them a Scrag they will not Relifh very well—Their are various conjectures with regard to Regulars leaving that Town, the Tories here I can fee are much fhagrin'd at it, and pretend to make the beft excufes poffibley for them, for my part I cannot help thinking but neciffity drove them from it, this is as glaring a proof as can be I think, that is that General Howe gave orders to Attack our lines, but Two Thoufand of his Men refuf'd (which guefs muft be the Men which were Order'd Under Lord Piercy, to attack Dorchefter Neck[2]) faying they had not forgot the Butchering of Bunker Hill, they fled fo precipately, that

---

[1] General Howe and the main army had evacuated the town of Bofton on the 17th of March, 1776. The reader will find a very complete account, both of the fiege and the evacuation of Bofton, in Mr. Frothingham's "Siege of Bofton," publifhed in Bofton in 1851.

[2] This paragraph probably refers to the movement of twenty-five hundred men, under the gallant Earl Percy, on the fifth of March, 1776. They were affembled at Caftle William, in boats, and were ordered to move againft the American lines, under cover of the night. Thefe preparations had been

the Officers had left their linnen & Watches in their Chambers, they will not come to This Town believe me till they are largely Reinforced—So much for thofe Hell Hounds

*   *   *   *   *   *

JNO. VARICK, JR., TO CAPT. RICHARD VARICK.

NEW YORK April 1ft, 1776—
Monday Morning

Dear Brother

*   *   *   *

In my laft I notified to you the Intentions of the 1ᵗ Batalion,[1] I may now inform you of what they have fince accomplifh'd. They have founded a Breaft-Work round the Hofpital[2] & almoft compleated it—com-

feen from the American camp; and the colonifts—already fenfible of their advantages—were eager for an opportunity to meet their enemy. Among the people in the neighborhood of the camp, alfo, the greateft excitement was produced, and thoufands flocked down to witnefs the expected battle.

Unfortunately for the gratification of the curious, *a terrible ftorm arofe* which continued two days, by which time General Wafhington had fo far perfected his defences that the projected attack was abandoned by General Howe. *Vide* Frothingham, pp. 299, 300.

[1] *Vide* note 2, page 71.

[2] The New York Hofpital originated in an organization of three phyficians —Doctors Middleton, John Jones, and Samuel Bard—in 1770; through whofe exertions a charter was obtained from the royal governor on the thirteenth July, 1776. The foundation of the building was laid on the twenty-feventh of July, 1773; but on the twenty-eighth of February, 1775, the ftill unfinifhed building was nearly deftroyed by fire.

The General Affembly granted £4000 toward rebuilding the edifice; but the war which followed prevented its completion until the third of January, 1791, when the firft patients were admitted.

12

pofed folely of Sod & Dirt—The Thicknefs of it about 10
Feet, & about 7 Feet high, with a Ditch of 12 Feet wide,
& 7 deep, furrounding the whole.—This will afford a fafe
Retreat, from the Fire of fmall Arms.—I have had the
Honor of working at it 3 or 4 Days, fince I enter'd the
Fiftileer Comp.ʸ under the Command of Capᵗ Livingfton.'—
The Fortification originates its Name from the Founders of
it, to wit, the 1ˢᵗ Batⁿ.—There is another Strucfure erecfed
on what formerly was called Byard's Mount, but now is
moftly term'd Bunckers Hill² & which when finifhed will
be a moft compleat Fort, and will command the whole
City.—I fine, every Ship is, & every Avennue leading from
the Water will be ftrongly fortified, to prevent our worft
of enemies from landing: & poffeffing themfelves of the
City, if they fhould ever attempt it.—But the Number of
Continental Troops that are to be ftation'd here, will I hope
prove fufficient to deter them from fuch an Attempt. There
are great Numbers daily arriving here, from all Quarters;
and it is univerfally thought, we will in a fhort Space of
Time, have an Army of 15,000 Men collecfed here for the
Prefervation of this City.—The People here do not feem
now fo apprehenfive of the Soldiers landing, fince the Ac-
count of the happy Fate of our Enemies evacuating the
City Bofton, on which I congratulate you & every other
Friend of Liberty.—The News of this happy Event feem'd

---

¹ *Vide* Note 1, page 72.

² Near the prefent corner of Broadway and Grand ftreet. *Vide* page 28.

to infpire the Breafts of every Friend to America with new
Hopes of Conquefts & with greater Ardor to refcue this
once flourifhing Country from the Shakles & Oppreffions
of a Britifh Parliament.—The Ships of War are the only
Tools we now apprehend any great Danger from, fince it
is out of our Power to cope with thofe thundering Hell
Hounds.   There is fome private Report that the minifterial
Mercinaries are now fortifying Bedlows Ifland, affifted by
many Countrymen.—if this can be relied on I doubt but
we will have a fmall Schirmifh there foon.

    *   *   *   *   *

JOHN VARICK, JR., TO CAPTAIN RICHARD VARICK.

NEW YORK May 14th 1776.

Dear Brother
            *   *

        The Tories are reduced to the Neceffity
of delivering up their Arms, & take an Oath, that they'll
refift every Attempt made by the Britifh Miniftry to violate
the rights & Liberties of America, or at leaft not affift them
in any of their fecreat Machinations.[1]   There are feveral

---

[1] The Continental Congrefs, on the fourteenth of March, 1776, had "re-
commended" to the feveral colonies, to caufe the "difaffected" within fuch
colonies to be difarmed; and to apply fuch arms to the arming of the troops
which fuch colonies might call into the fervice.

On the twenty-fixth of March, the Committee of Safety referred this re-
folution of "recommendation" above referred to, to a committee of two
members—Meffrs. Tredwell and Moore—who, on the next day, reported a plan of operations for carrying the fame into effect; with the addi-

who refuſe to take the Oath : leaſt they ſhould perjure themſelves.—From this it is infer'd that they have ſigned & ſwore to ſome Decleration ; And the Congreſs has ta-ken the Method of ſecuring all ſuch Perſons in Priſon, for yeſterday John Roome Att⁷ & Auguſtus Van Horne was carried to Jail on that Acc⁴ & doubtleſs there will be many more ere long.—There is ſome Proſpect now of diſcovering all thoſe vile Raſcals, that have already paſſ'd too long un-noticed, & have enjoy'd greater Benifits than their bleed-ing Countrymen.—There will ſoon be a ſtop to this Tory Faction.   *   *   *   *   *

The Granadiers¹ have gain'd themſelves great Honor, by their erecting the circular Battery nominated after them : For they rec⁴ the Thanks of Gen¹ Sterling² in a moſt pub-lick Manner.—It is of real Satiſtaction to Me to think that a few of our Citizens have behaved in ſuch a Manner, as has redounded to their Honor. And hope it may prove a

tional proviſion that the parties who were to be thus diſarmed ſhould alſo be compelled to ſign a paper called an "aſſociation," promiſing "to defend by arms, the United American Colonies againſt the hoſtile attempts of the Britiſh fleets and armies, until the preſent unhappy controverſy between the two countries ſhall be ſettled"—a promiſe which, when made, was generally made under ſtreſs of circumſtances, and was obeyed only, as might have been ex-pected, while the peculiar circumſtances which produced the promiſe con-tinued to operate.

¹ This company wore a uniform of blue, with red facings, and was com-manded by Colonel John Laſher, as captain, William Hyer, as firſt lieutenant, Abraham Braſher, as ſecond lieutenant, and Abraham Van Dyck, as third lieutenant.

² Vide Note 5, page 86.

Means to clear up the Imputation & Contempt this City was held in by fome of the Neighbouring Colonies.

*　　*　　*　　*　　*　　*

PETER ELTING TO CAPT. RICHARD VARICK.

New York 4th June 1776

Dear Brother

*　　*　　*　　*　　*

Time will hardly admit to add any news. Coll. Putnam[1] tells me that there ware Seven armed Veffels at the hook yefterday, Small & Large, our Congrefs have laid a plan to block up the Harbour, But are waiting to lay there plan before Gen¹ Wafhington, who is Expected back from Philadelphia this Evening[2], Two fmall french Veffels ar-

---

[1] Colonel Rufus Putnam, a coufin of the general of that name, but a much more ufeful man.

He was an excellent engineer, and poffeffed the entire confidence of the commander-in-chief, of which he was eminently worthy, and which he never forfeited.

After the war was over, he removed to the North-weft, and was one of the pioneer fettlers of Ohio—making his home at Marietta. He was a judge of the United States Court, a brigadier general of the army, during the adminiftration of Prefident Wafhington, and furveyor general of the United States. He was a member of the Conftitutional Convention of Ohio, in 1802; the firft grand mafter of the Mafonic fraternity in Ohio; and in 1812, one of the founders of the firft Bible Society weft of the Alleghanies. He died in May, 1824, aged eighty-feven years.

[2] "Congrefs having been pleafed to requeft my attendance at Philadelphia, to advife with them on the fituation of our affairs, and of fuch meafures as may be proper for works of Defence."—*General Wafhington to General Schuyler*, 22 May, 1776.

ived here yefterday & they fay five more are on there way
near by. Loaded with. Brandy Indigo. Sugers. Molaffes &c
—We Expect a fleet & army Here foon. our Batteries are
fo farr Ready that I am In hopes they will meet with a
much warmer Reception than they think for. what other
news We have you will find in the prints

*   *   *

P. S. I have got you the only pr Piftels to be found I
hope they may fute you the price is 80/ pr I fend them by
the bearer

SOLOMON DROWNE, M. D., TO SOLOMON DROWNE, SR.

NEW YORK June 4th 1776.

Hond Sir.

Amidft a good deal of hurry and Noife I fet
down to write you a few Lines (tho' late at Night) by Mr J.
Brown, who fets away Tomorrow.

We arrived here yefterday.   *   *   *   a little after ten.

*   *   *   *

We waited on Doct Morgan[1] to Day, and were kindly received. He marked out a Courfe of Duty for us at the
Hofpital which will keep us very bufy. The College is
occupied for the General Hofpital. It is a very elegant
Building. and its Situation pleafant. and falubrious. We

" *Ordered,* That General Wafhington attend in Congrefs to-morrow."—
Journals of Congrefs, May 23, 1776.

[1] Doctor John Morgan, who was Director General and Phyfician-in-chief
to the General Hofpital of the American army.

were fhown the Apartment allotted us in it to Day, which we like very well; and expect to move from the place we put up at, tomorrow.—I have a Lift of Medicines, purchafed here for yᵉ Continental Hofpital, to copy for Docᵗ Morgan, which obliges me to conclude.

*   *   *   *

JOHN VARICK, JR., TO CAPTAIN RICHARD VARICK.

New York June 10ᵗʰ 1776 Monday.

Dear Brother

*   *   *   *

The Tories here feem'd to exult in their Opinion, that General Wafhington was gone to Philadelphia in Order to refign his Commiffion, if the Congrefs declar'd for an Independence. It was even currently reported, that he was gone with that View.—How was the Torie's Exultations & Wifhes fruftrated on his Return.—they can make no Reply to what they alledged at his Departure[1].

To what low Means do our Enemies already ftoop, & what unjuftifiable, & mean Methods do they purfue to obtain the Inteligence they daily receive of our Motions; for yefterday was taken up in this City, and carried to Goal, a Negro Fellow who belong'd to Col Jenning, & a free Negro, who had been employed in a Peauger, to carry Provifions on Board of the Governors Ship[2], from here, & fuch

---

[1] *Vide* Note 2, page 93.

[2] Governor Tryon was, at that period, on board the fhip *Duchefs of Gordon*, at anchor in the harbor.

Inteligence as they, & their Accomplices in this City could collect, for the Information of that vile Rascal, on Board the Dutches of Gordon. There is a Letter now in Town in the Name of Pitt,[1] attested as a true Copy from the Original by W. T. which protests against the Proceedings of the Colonies, & imports that as long as we contended for Liberty, he was our Friend, but since we had levy'd open War against his Majesty, every Sinew, & every Nerve shou'd be exerted to suppress Rebellion, & reduce his Subjects to a Sense of their Duty. It is believ'd, it has been contriv'd & fabricated on Board of the Dutches of Gordon (since it first came from there, to be distributed about by the Tories;) under the Name of Pitt, in Order to discourage the People. It is to be hoped however, that it will not be attended with such evil Consequences, as might be apprehended from it if really true, But the Veracity of it is suspected on Grounds of Probability—These are most unhappy Times, when we are reduced to such Straits; as that Persons, who were once considered as Patriots to their Country, will descend so far beneath the Character, & Dignity of Gentlemen, as to pursue the Vilest of Measures, & consider nothing to mean to act if they can only perpetrate their wicked, & detestible Desires.

*

[1] Lord Chatham had been an early and devoted friend to the American Colonies; and such a letter as that which is here described would have been very beneficial to the royal cause.

PETER ELTING TO CAPT. RICHARD VARICK.

NEW YORK 13th June 1776

Dear Brother

*

We Had fome Grand Toory Rides in this City this week, & in particular Yefterday, Several of them ware handeld verry Roughly Being Caried trugh the Streets on Rails, there Cloaths Tore from there becks and there Bodies pritty well Mingled with the duft.[1] Amongft them ware C—— Capt. Hardenbrook,[2] Mr. Rapelje,[3] Mr. Queen the Poticary & Leflly the barber. There is hardly a toory face to be feen this morning—Our Congrefs publifhed a Refolve on the Ocafion, Exprefling there difaprobation, tho it might have procedid from a Proper Zeal for the liberties of Amarican freedom & defire that it may Ceafe, & that a mode for punifhing fuch Offenders will foon be adopted for this Colony[4]

*   *

[1] " —— have been cruelly rode on rails, a practice moft painful, dangerous, and, till now, peculiar to the humane republicans of New England."—*Letter from Staten Ifland, Auguft* 17, cited in Moore's " Diary of the American Revolution."

[2] Theophilus Hardenbrook.

[3] Rem Rapelje.

[4] " Generals Putnam and Mifflin having complained to this Congrefs of the riotous and diforderly conduct of numbers of the inhabitants of this city, which had led, this day, to acts of violence towards fome difaffected perfons : it was thereupon

"*Refolved*, That this Congrefs by no means approve of the riots that have happened this day ; they flatter themfelves, however, that they have proceeded from a real regard to liberty and a deteftation of thofe perfons who,

SOLOMON DROWNE, M. D., TO SOLOMON DROWNE, SENR.

GENERAL HOSPITAL, N. YORK June 17th [1776]

Hon^d Sir,

At length I am fomewhat fettled to what I
have been fince my arrival here. The Quarter-Mafter of
ye Hofpital and his Wife reached here a few Days paft,
from Bolton; fince which we live in a very elegant Manner, compared with what we did. As there happened to
be fome Vacancies in the Hofpital, I have as good a Berth
as I cou'd have wifhed for. (The fame as Mr Binney's.)[1]
We draw Twenty Dollars a Month, and Two Rations P^r
Day. I have enjoyed a good ftate of Health fince I have
been here. We have been clofely employed a good part
of ye time, affifting in putting up Medicines for thirty
Chefts. By the Paper I fend inclofed, you will fee we
expect an Attack this way foon. 'Tis thought they will
attempt landing on Long-Ifland, by fome:—by others, that
they will, with a fair breeze, run by the forts, up North
River and land. We have things in pretty good Readi-

by their language and conduct, have difcovered themfelves to be inimical to
the caufe of America. To urge the warm friends of liberty to decency and
good order, this Congrefs affures the public that effectual meafures fhall be
taken to fecure the enemies of American liberty in this colony ; and do require the good people of this city and colony to defift from all riots, and
leave the offenders againft fo good a caufe to be dealt with by the conftitutional reprefentatives of the colony."—*Journal of Provincial Congrefs*,
June 12, 1776.

[1] This Mr. Binney is the gentleman to whom Dr. Drowne often refers when
fpeaking of " us" and " we."

nefs at the Hofpital for the horrid Effects of a general Action. I hope it may not come to this; but that the fchemes of our Enemies may be fruftrated.

A part of ye Artillery Regt and a Number of Volunteers have gone upon an Expedition down ye River to ye Narrows, I believe; to take ye watering place from ye Afia's Men, or drive ye Regulars from their fort at ye Light-Houfe, and deftroy it.

There has lately been a good deal of attention paid the Tories in this City. Some of the worft have been carried thro' the ftreets (at Noonday) on Rails, &c.   *   *

PETER ELTING TO CAPT. RICHARD VARICK.

NEW YORK 9th July 1776.

Dear Brother

           *

Your Shoes I could not git for you on account of the Alarm on the arival of the fleet,[1] fince which almoft all bufinefs in town is knocked up the Fleet now lays verry Quiet at the watering Place[2], waiting for a Reanforcement from England[3] When they fay they fhall little Regard

---

[1] The fleet from Halifax, having on board the Britifh army under Sir William Howe, arrived at Sandy Hook on the twenty-ninth of June; and the troops were debarked on the fecond and third of July.

[2] Near the prefent Quarantine.

[3] Then on its way from England; arriving at New York on the twelfth of Auguft, 1776.

our Bateries We as little Regard them, Our men are in high Sperrits and Ready to meet them at any Hour the town fwarms with people, I doubt not But our army Confifts of at leaft twenty thoufand men, & the Country about us verry Willing to lend us there afiftence, I am verry Sorry to hear fo much of the bed fuccefs of the Army in your quarter,[1] I am afraid it will Be Attended with bed Confiquences   *   *   *   *   *   *

SOLOMON DROWNE, M. D., TO MISS SALLY DROWNE.

GENERAL HOSPITAL N. YORK July 13th [1776]

Dear Sifter Sally,
         *   *

I fuppofe you will have heard before this reaches you, that y[e] Fleet has arrived here, and lies in fair view of y[e] City. Yefter-Afternoon two Ships & three Tenders came to fail, and ftood towards y[e] City. They had not got fairly within fhot, before our Forts & Batteries began to fire at them:—and, what was mortifying, they kept fteadily along feemingly regardlefs of our conftant fire, till they got almoft abreaft of our Works; then gave us a few paffing Brodfides, and, with a fine Breeze, failed ftatelyly up North River, I believe unhurt by us.

But, fhocking to tell, we had fix fine fellows killed & 4

---

[1] The Northern army had retired from Canada, and taken poft at Crown Point. It was very fickly; and great numbers were fuffering from the fmall-pox.

or five wounded at our Grand Battery, thro' mere Carelefs-
nefs, or Ignorance. For, neglecting to fwab ye Cannon at
all, or doing it improperly, the catridges took fire, and ye
fatal Accidents enfued.

The Wounded were brought to ye Hofpital, and this
day one of them had his Arm (all ye Bones of which were
broken) taken off. He was *moved* firft to the new or City
Hofpital, which has been intended & fitted for ye wounded:
where I now attend him to be ready if ye ftump fhou'd
bleed affrefh. One Ball came into ye Hofpital Yard, ftruck
ye ground at a little Diftance from us, and bounded thro'
ye board fence I believe it was a 12 pound fhott. I think
our fituation as much expofed, as any in the City.

    ✻   ✻   ✻

I am glad our Affembly have allowed of Inoculation,
and hope you & Bro' Bill will not defer receiving *that
Difeafe*, (ye s. Pox[1]) *which* taken by chance has proved ye
Bane of tens of Thoufands; when it comes fo near you,
cloathed in Gentlenefs,—all its Terriblenefs caft afide.

My Sifter, I congratulate you, and ye reft of ye Family,
that ye live in a Free and Independent Country,—The
United States of America.

            ✻

There exifted confiderable difference of opinion among even well informec.
ficians as to the advantages refulting from inoculation.

PETER ELTING TO CAPT. RICHARD VARICK.

NEW YORK 17th July 1776

Dr Brother

*   *   *   *   *

We Expect An Attack from the menwarr
Every moment, the troops I imagin wonte Come to make
any attempt until they are reinforced, Lord How is arrived
but brought none,[1] two Menwarr have gone up the North
River laſt friday as high as tappen[2]   they met with Conſiderable damage,[3] & yeſterday they have gone up to Haver-
ſtraw,[4] I fency they meen to go up as high as poughkeepſy
to diſtroy our two Veſſels a building[5] (if they do I am in
hopes our foorts In the Highlands[6] will ſave them the
truble of Coming Back, Our Army is in high Sperrits and
are all Wiſhing for an Attack from the Enimy, We Rec^d
No damage from the Enimies fiering laſt fryday[7] Only one
Cow killed which made good market Beef   But ſix of our

[1] Lord Howe, in the *Eagle*, arrived at New York on the evening of the
twelfth of July; and the reinforcements did not arrive until the twelfth of
Auguſt.

[2] The Roſe and the Phœnix, with three tenders, moved up the river on
the afternoon of the twelfth of July.—*General Waſhington's Letter to the
Preſident of Congreſs*, July 12, 1776.

[3] The amount of damage really done was probably ſmaller than this letter
would appear to indicate. They ſuffered no apparent injury.—*Sparks'
Waſhington*, III., p. 475, note.

[4] "Sparks' Waſhington," III., p. 475, note.

[5] Two frigates were then on the ſtocks at Poughkeepſie.

[6] Forts Montgomery and Clinton.

[7] *Vide* pages 100, 101.

train got killed & four or five Wounded from being over
Zealous, not taken proper time to fwadd the guns, We
hear Near fourty got killed on board the fhips[1]—two flags
have Bean fent by Lord *howe* to George Wafhington &c &c
&c Which ware both fent back, Or Reather Refufed for
not being properly deracted,[2] I am happy Your Northern
Army has made fo fafe a Retreat[3] I am in Great hopes we
fhall be a match for them Here

     *   *   *   *   *

PETER ELTING TO CAPT. RICHARD VARICK.

NEW YORK 30th July 1776

Dear Brother

            *   *   *

You would be furprifed to fe what Num-
ber of Empty houfes here are in this place, Verry few of the
inhabitents Remain in town that are not ingaged in the Service[4]   *   *   *   *   *   *

Great preparations are making here With Shiver de
freefes and Veffels to ftop up the Channel,[5] & fundry fire

---

[1] There is little reafon to fuppofe that the lofs was near as great as is here
reprefented. Three were wounded on the *Rofe;* and the lofs of the *Phœnix*
is unknown.

[2] *Vide* General Wafhington's Letters to Prefident of Congrefs, July 14 and
17, 1776.

[3] *Vide* Note 1, page 100.

[4] *Vide* Butler's Statement. (*Tomlinfon MSS.*)

[5] "I am preparing fome obftructions for the channel nearly oppofite the
works at the upper end of the ifland."—*General Wafhington to Prefid nt of*

ships, preparing   two Brigs are Ready,[1] fomthing great will
Be attempted foon, five or feven Rogallies are already come
down from the Eaftward   two are built here that will carry
one 32 Pounder Each, One of them quite and the other
Nearly finished,[2] the fleet Remains Verry Quiet, But the
men of the two menwar Up the River have a fmall brufh
Once in a While with our Guards long the River[3]

　　　※　　　　　　　　　※　　　　　　　　　※

SOLOMON DROWNE, M. D., TO SOLOMON DROWNE, SENR.

NEW YORK Auguft 9th [1776.]

Hon^d Parents,

　　　※

Yefter-Morning before two o'Clock we were alarmed:—
however, it turn'd out no more, than that a Number of
the Enemy's Boats came up towards ye City.   Surely we
have no defpicable Enemy to deal with;—brought up to

Congrefs, 25 July, 1776.   See alfo his letter to the fame gentleman, Auguft
5, 1776, and "General Heath's Memoirs," Auguft 1.

A tolerably complete account of thefe obftructions has been written by
Mr. Ruttenber; and publifhed by J. Munfell, in his "Hiftorical Series."

[1] A Mr. Anderfon had propofed a plan for the deftruction of the enemy's
fleet by means of firefhips; and he had been employed, under the direction
of General Wafhington, in conftructing them.

[2] *Vide* General Wafhington's letter to Prefident of Congrefs, July 29,
1776; and "General Heath's Memoirs," July 25 and 28, and Auguft 1.

[3] "*Aug.* 3.   About noon there was a brifk cannonade up the Hudfon, between the American row-galleys and the Britifh fhips: the former had two
men killed; two mortally, and 12 flightly wounded.   The Britifh lofs was
not known."—*Heath's Memoirs.*

War;—their officers well skilled in yᵉ Military Art;—their Bands well disciplined;—they are formidable: But they have the Hessians, &c. for *their Allies*, for whose Aid the British Coffers (some of them at least) must be emptied.

We, for *our Ally*, have the *Great GOD*,—who, requires no subsidy,—nought, save a grateful Mind and a right Fear of *Him;* and to conduct with true Integrity.

Our Wages were raised some time ago (in consequence of a Petition to Congress) to thirty Dollars Pᵉ Month, or a Dollar pᵉ Day. The Pay wou'd be no Inducement to stay a moment in this shocking Place, at the Expense of Health, that best of Blessings. The Air of the whole City seems infected. In almost every street there is a horrid smell.— But, Duty to my Country, and another Consideration, require, that I shou'd not quit my Post at this Juncture.

❋   ❋   ❋   ❋   ❋   ❋

PETER ELTING TO CAPT. RICHARD VARICK.

HACKENSACK 12th Sepʳ 1776

Dear Brother

This is the verry first opertunity I had to send you a line since my return, we got back yesterday a week, and my Curiosity has since led me to town three times, tho To Little satisfaction, the town Apears to me to be in a Bad state of defance it seems the greatest depandence Is made on the muskitry But am informed that our army is in a much better Posture of defence at Hornshook[1]

---

[1] Horen's Hook—now called "Harris's Point"—nearly opposite Hurlgate.

14

and Kingsbridge, at the later the grand ſtand is to be made Many Waggons & Horſes about here have been Impres for Carrying the ſtores, Proviſions &c out of New York I donte doubt but you have a much better account of the Battles and Vacuation of long Iſland[1] then I am able to give you the Enimy have Erected a bomb and two Attilery battiries over again ours at Horns Hook[2], which has ocaſioned an almoſt Conſtant Cannonading for a weak, with Little loſs of blodd on our ſide, which was one men killed & another Wounded yeſterday, I doubt not but a ſevere blow will Be ſtruck ſoon—Its Currently Reported ſince Genl Sullivan's Return from Congreſs[3] that three of the

[1] The Battle of Long Iſland was fought on the twenty-eighth of Auguſt, 1776; and on the night of the twenty-ninth the army evacuated the iſland.

The battle has been fully deſcribed in the letters of Colonel Harriſon to the Preſident of Congreſs, 27 Auguſt; of Lord Sterling to General Waſhington, Auguſt 29; of Colonel Haſlett to Thomas Rodney, October 4, 1776; of General Sullivan to the Preſident of Congreſs, October 25, 1777; of General Howe to Lord George Germain, 3d September; in "Thompſon's Long Iſland," I., pp. 196, 214, 222; in Mr. Ward's paper on that ſubject before the New York Hiſtorical Society; in Dawſon's "Battles of the United States," I., pp. 143-159, etc.

The "Evacuation" of Long Iſland, as it is here called, has been deſcribed fully in General Waſhington's letters to the Preſident of Congreſs, Auguſt 31, 1776, and that to his brother, John Auguſtine, 22 September, 1776; Marſhall's "Waſhington" (4to Edit.), II., p. 439; Gordon's "Revolution" (London, 1788), II., pp. 312-316; and Stedman, I., pp. 197-8.

[2] Vide Note 1, page 105.

[3] General Sullivan, who had been taken priſoner at Long Iſland, had been diſpatched to Philadelphia, by order of Admiral Lord Howe, to invite, in his behalf, a conference for the purpoſe of attempting to adjuſt the differences between the United States and Great Britain.

Members are to have a Confirence with Lord & Gen¹ How, they ware this day to meet at amboy on the Ocafion¹   Our army is ftill in high fpirits and Willing to meet their foes at any hour.

❋

¹ The meeting between Lord Howe and the three members here referred to—Meffrs. Franklin, John Adams, and Rutledge—took place at the "Billop Houfe," on Staten Ifland, on the eleventh of September, full reports of which may be found in the Journals of the Continental Congrefs, September 17, 1776; in Lord Howe's letter to Lord George Germain, September 20, 1776; the "Works of Doctor Franklin" (*Bofton*, 1840), V., pp. 97–108, VIII., p. 187; General Wafhington's letters to Prefident of Congrefs, 31 Auguft, and 8 September, 1776; "Autobiography of John Adams" (*Works*, III., pp. 75–79), John Adams to James Warren, September 8, and the fame to Samuel Adams, fame date and September 17, 1776.

THE BATTLE OF HARLEM PLAINS.

[The following letter, written a few days after the affair, relates principally to the action on the Harlem plains, September 16th, 1776. That engagement, whether confidered in its origin, or the manner in which it was conducted, or in its effect on both armies, was one of the moft important of the minor actions of the War of the Revolution.

Other accounts of the action may be found in letters of General Wafhington to the Prefident of Congrefs, September 18, 1776, and to John Auguftine Wafhington, September 22, 1776; General Greene's letter to Governor Cooke, September 17, 1776; Colonel Reed's letter to his wife, (Life of Jos. Reed, I., pp. 237–239;) Lofling's Field Book, II., pp. 612, 613; and Dawfon's Battles of the United States, I., pp. 160–166.

George Clinton, the writer, was born in Orange county, New York, July 26, 1739. His early life was one of adventure, and he fubfequently ftudied law with William Smith.

In 1775, he was a member of the General Affembly of the Colony, and difplayed great firmnefs in his oppofition to the government. On the 15th of May, 1775, he took his feat in the Continental Congrefs, and voted for Independence in July, 1776, although he was called into the field before the engroffed copy of the Declaration had been prepared for fignature, and his name does not appear on it. In March, 1777, he was commiffioned a brigadier-general in the Continental army, having occupied a fimilar poft in the New York fervice many months before that time. In April, 1777, he was chofen *both Governor and Lieutenant-Governor of New York*, and accepted the former; to which office he was re-elected five terms—in all eighteen years.

When the enemy moved up the Hudfon, in October, 1777, he prorogued the Affembly, and, with his brother James, threw himfelf into Fort Montgomery, which he defended with the moft defperate bravery, abandoning the works only when the enemy had completely captured them.

He prefided in the Convention of New York, which confidered and ratified the Conftitution of the United States; in 1801, he was re-elected governor; and, in 1804, Vice-Preſident of the United States, which office he held until his deceaſe.

He died April 20, 1812, aged ſeventy-two years.]

GEN. GEO. CLINTON'S LETTER.

KING'S BRIDGE 21ſt Sepr 1776.

Dr Doctor

I was favoured with yours by Capt. Jack-ſon wrote at my Houſe Eight Days ago for which I am much oblidged to you as it realy relieved me of great anx-iety reſpecting Ceaty's Health[1] which I however yet fear is in a declining ſtate. Your brother too I hear lays very Ill at my Houſe with a Fevour which gives me great Concern. I have been ſo hurried & Fatigued out of the ordinary way of my Duty by the Removal of our Army from New York[2] & great Part of the public ſtores to this Place that it has almoſt worn me out tho' as to Health I am as well as uſual; but how my Conſtitution has been able to ſtand lying out ſeveral Nights in the Open Air & expoſed to Rain is almoſt a Miracle to me—Whom at Home the leaſt Wet indeed ſome Times the Change of Weather almoſt laid me up.

The Evacuation of the City I ſuppoſe has much alarmed the Country. It was judged untenable in Council of Genl Officers conſidering the Enemy poſſeſſed of Long-Iſland &c

---

[1] "Ceaty"—Mrs. Catharine Livingſton, wife of Gilbert Livingſton and ſiſter of Mrs. Tappan.

[2] The evacuation of New York by the Americans, September 15, 1776.

and was therefore advifed to be evacuated.[1] The Artillery (at leaft all worth moving) & allmoft all the public ftores were removed out of it[2] fo that when the Enemy landed & attacked our Lines near the City[3] we had but few Men there (thofe indeed did not behave well[4]) our Lofs however by our Retreat from there either in Men or Stores is very

[1] "I called one (a Council) on the 12th, when a large majority not only determined a removal of the army prudent, but abfolutely neceffary, declaring that they were entirely convinced from a full and minute enquiry into our fituation that it was extremely perilous."—General Wafhington to Prefident of Congrefs, 14 September, 1776.

[2] General Clinton evidently was in error in this remark. Jos. Trumbull, commiffary-general, writing to the Convention of New York, ("King's Bridge, September 16, 1776,") fays, "In the retreat, I have been obliged to leave behind large quantities of flour, which reduces our magazine too low. It is abfolutely neceffary to have a large quantity foon." General Wafhington, alfo, (Letter to Congrefs, September 16, 1776) fays, "Moft of our heavy cannon, a confiderable part of our baggage, and a part of our ftores and provifions, which we were about removing, were unavoidably left in the city."

[3] Between Turtle Bay and the city, September 15, 1776.

[4] "To my great furprize and mortification, I found the troops that had been pofted in the lines retreating with the utmoft precipitation, and thofe ordered to fupport them (Parfons's and Fellows's brigades) flying in every direction, and in the greateft confufion, notwithftanding the exertions of their generals to form them. I ufed every means in my power to rally and get them into fome order; but my attempts were fruitlefs and ineffectual; and on the appearance of a fmall party of the enemy, not more than fixty or feventy, their diforder increafed, and they ran away in the greateft confufion without firing a fingle fhot."—General Wafhington to Prefident of Congrefs, 16 September, 1776. The brigades of Parfons and Fellows referred to, embraced eight regiments of Connecticut troops, and both the American officers and thofe of the enemy agree in their defcriptions of the bad conduct of the above troops.

inconfiderable.[1] I would not be underftood that it was my Oppinion to evacuate the City[2] neither do I mean now to condemn the Meafure it is done intended for the beft I am certain.

The fame Day the Enemy poffeffed themfelves of the City, to wit, laft Sunday they landed the Main Body of their Army & encamped on York Ifland acrofs about the Eight Mile Stone & between that & the four Mile Stone.[3] Our Army at leaft one Divifion of it lay at Col⁰ Morris's[4] & fo fouthward to near the Hollow Way which runs acrofs from Harlem Flat to the North River at Matje Davit's Fly[5]

[1] *Vide* Note 4, page 110.

[2] The generals prefent in the Council who oppofed the propofed evacuation of the city, were Spencer, Clinton, and Heath. General Mercer, alfo, was oppofed to the evacuation, although he was not prefent in the Council which had advifed it.

[3] The eighth mile-ftone on the old Bofton road, meafured from the old City Hall in Wall ftreet, muft not be confounded with the eighth mile-ftone on the prefent roads running north from the city. The former was, probably, near the prefent fuburban village of Yorkville.

[4] "*Col. Morris's.*"—Richard Morris had ferved in the French war, where he had been one of the aides of General Braddock. He married Mary Phillipfe, daughter of the lord of the manor of Phillipfe, in Weftchefter county, and fettled in New York at the clofe of the war; and fubfequently he became a member of the Council of the Province. On the reftoration of peace, he went to England, where he died in 1794, aged fixty-feven years; his widow, well known as one of General Wafhington's moft intimate early friends, furvived him until 1825, when fhe died, aged ninety-fix.

The country-feat of Mr. Morris here referred to, and, at the date of this letter, the head-quarters of General Wafhington, is ftill ftanding, about ten miles from the city; and is well known as the refidence of Madame Jumel, the widow of Aaron Burr.

[5] Maretje Davit's Vly—a low fwampy fpot, a little weft from the Eighth

About half way between which two Places our Lines run
acrofs the River which indeed at that Time were only began
but are now in a very defenfible ftate. On Monday Morning the Enemy attacked our Advanced Party Commanded
Colº Knowlton[1] (a brave Officer who was killed in the
Action) near the Point of Matje Davit's Fly the Fire was
very brifk on both fides our People however foon drove
them back into a Clear Field about 200 Paces South Eaft
of that where they lodged themfelves behind a Fence covered with Bufhes our People purfued them but being ob-

avenue, near One hundred and twenty-fourth ftreet. This locality, in earlier periods, was fomewhat celebrated as one of the landmarks between the
two ancient corporations of New York and Harlem.

[1] Colonel Thomas Knowlton was born at Ipfwich, Maffachufetts, about the
year 1740; and having been left an orphan at an early age, he entered the
army, under Captain Ifrael Putnam, in 1755, and ferved on the northern
frontiers during fix campaigns, with great credit. He was alfo engaged in
the expedition againft Cuba, in 1762; and was prefent at the capture of
Havana. On the opening of hoftilities in 1775, he was elected to the command of the Afhford company; and he was among the firft to reach Maffachufetts, in that exciting ftruggle.

He was the commander of the Connecticut troops in the battle of Bunker's
Hill, June 17, 1775, winning imperifhable renown; foon after which he was
promoted to the rank of Major, and, at the clofe of the year he retired to Connecticut. In 1776, he returned to the fervice with the rank of lieutenant-
colonel, commanding a corps of rangers; and he fecured the entire confidence of General Wafhington and of the army.

When the Connecticut troops, at Kip's Bay, had brought fo much difgrace
on their ftate, he thirfted for an opportunity to wipe off the ftain; and the
refult of his afpirations was the fpirited affair which has been defcribed in this
letter. He fell, nobly, on the Harlem Plains, as herein related; and he was
buried in the trenches at Fort Wafhington, where his remains ftill reft,
without a ftick or a ftone to mark the fpot.

lidged to ſtand expoſed in the open Field or take a Fence at a Conſiderable Diſtance they preferred the Latter it was indeed adviſeable for we ſoon brought a Couple of Field Pieces to bear upon them which fairly put them to Flight with two Diſcharges only the Second Time our People purſued them cloſely to the Top of a Hill about 400 paces diſtant where they received a very Conſiderable Reinforcement & made their Second Stand Our People alſo had received a Conſiderable Reinforcement, and at this Place a very briſk Action commenced which continued for near two Hours in which Time we drove the Enemy into a Neighbouring orchard from that acroſs a Hollow & up another Hill not far Diſtant from their own Encampment, here we found the Ground rather Diſadvantageous & a Retreat inſecure we therefore thot proper not to purſue them any farther & retired to our firſt Ground leaving the Enemy on the laſt Ground we drove them to'—That Night I commanded the Right Wing of our advanced Party or Picket on the Ground the Action firſt began of which Col° Pawling[2]

[1] Detailed accounts of this action—known as *the Battle of Harlem Plains*—in General Waſhington's letter to Congreſs, September 18, 1776; his letter to his brother, John Auguſtine, September 22, 1776; his letter to Governor Cooke, September 17, 1776; General Greene's letter to Governor Cooke, of the ſame date; Colonel Joſeph Reed's letter to his wife, *Life*, I., pp. 237–239; Dawſon's Battles of the United States, I., pp. 160–162; Loſſing's Field Book, II., pp. 817–819; Dunlap's New York, II., pp. 77, 78.

[2] Colonel Levi Pawling, of Marbletown, commanded a regiment of Ulſter county militia (*Jour. of Prov. Convention*, July 17, 1776). He had been a member of the Provincial Congreſs; in May, 1777, was appointed Firſt

& Col° Nicoll's[1] Regiment were part and next Day I fent a Party to bury our Dead. They found but 17. The Enemy removed theirs in the Night we found above 60 Places where dead Men had lay from Pudles of Blood & other appearances & at other Places fragments of Bandages & Lint.[2] From the beft Account our Lofs killed & wounded is not much lefs than feventy feventeen of which only dead[3] [this Account of our Lofs exceeds what I mentioned in a Letter I wrote Home indeed at that Time I only had an account of the Dead—the Wounded were removed—12 oclock M. Sunday two Deferters from on Board the Bruno Man of War[4] lying at Morifiaina fay the Enemy had 300 killed on Monday laft. *Note by Gen. Clinton.*] the Reft moftly likely do well & theirs is fomewhere about 300— upwards it is generally believed—Tho I was in the latter

Judge of Ulfter county; and was, alfo, a fenator in 1777 and 1782. He died in 1782.—(*Coll. of Ulfter Hift. Soc., I., p. 162.*)

[1] Colonel Ifaac Nicoll, of Gofhen, Orange county, had commanded the regiment of "Minute-men in Orange County," (*Jour. of Com. of Safety, Jan. 5, 1776*) but at the period referred to in this letter, he commanded a regiment of Orange county militia (*Jour. of Prov. Convention, July 17, 1776*).

[2] The lofs of the enemy has never been fatiffactorily afcertained, as the reports have been concealed, or fo much divided as to miflead the ftudent. There is no doubt that the lofs was confiderably over three hundred—the heavieft lofs falling on the Light Infantry.

[3] The lofs of the Americans, "in killed and wounded, was about fixty; but the greateft lofs we fuftained was in the death of Lieutenant-Colonel Knowlton, a brave and gallant officer."—*General Wafhington to John Auguftine Wafhington, 22 September, 1776.*

[4] "*Bruno.*"—La Brune.

Part indeed almoſt the whole of the Action I did not think ſo many Men were engaged It is without Doubt however they had out on the Occaſion between 4 & 5000 of their choiſeſt Troops[1] & expected to have drove us off the Iſland. They are greatly mortified at their Diſapointment & have ever ſince been exceedingly modeſt & quiet not having even pratroling Parties beyond their Lines—I lay within a Mile of them the Night after the battle & never heard Men work harder I believe they thought we intended to purſue our Advantage & Attack them next Morning.

If I only had a Pair of Piſtols I coud I think have ſhot a Raſcal or two I am ſure I woud at leaſt have ſhot a puppy of an Officer I found ſlinking off in the heat of the Action[2] it is a pitty yours ſhould lay idle—Had I my ſword I coud change it much to my Liking in which Caſe I woud Return yours—Do my dear Doctor call & ſee your ſiſter as often as you poſſibly can & let me hear from you as often as opportunity offers—My Love to my Brother & believe me

Your's

Sincerely

GEO CLINTON

Sunday 22d Sepr. Night before laſt about one oClock

[1] The number of the enemy, alſo, is unknown. There is reaſon to ſuppoſe, however, that it was not leſs than a thouſand, excluſive of the covering party.

[2] An inſtance of this "ſlinking off," in this action, may be found recorded in the minutes of the General Court Martial, in the caſe of Ebenezer Leſſing-well of Colonel Durkee's regiment, September 19, 1776.

there was a terrible Fire towards the City   it occafioned remarkable Light at this Place.   It continued till yefterday
afternoon   by accounts from Paulus Hook[1] which is yet in
our Poffeffion it was in the City, broke out in fundry Places
at the fame Time & is great Part confumed.[2]   There is a
flying Report of a French & Spanifh Fleet to the Southward & it is faid 7 of the largeft fhipping left N York yefterday how true I cant fay.   I have not time to write
Home   You muft go fee them.

[Addreffed to

Doctor Peter Tappen[3]

at

Fort Montgomery.]

[1] "*Paulus Hook*"—now Jerfey City.

[2] The "terrible fire" here referred to, broke out "at or near Whitehall, foon
extended to the Exchange, took its courfe up the weft fide of Broad-ftreet, as
far as Verlattenberg Hill, confuming all the blocks from the Whitehall up.
The flames extended acrofs the Broadway from the houfe of Mr. David
Johnfton to Beaver Lane, or Fincher's Alley, on the weft, and carried all before it, a few buildings excepted, to the houfe at the corner of Barcley-ftreet,
wherein the late Mr. Adam Vandenberg lived, fweeping all the crofs ftreets
in the way.   The buildings left ftanding, on the weft fide of the Broadway, are
fuppofed to be Captain Thomas Randall's, Capt. Kennedy's, Dr. Mallat's,
Mr. John Cortlandt's fugar houfe and dwelling houfe, Dr. Jones's, Hull's
tavern, St. Paul's, Mr. Axtell's, and Mr. Rutherford's.   The caufe of the
fire is not known.   We imagine about a 6th part of the whole city is deftroyed, and many families have loft their All."—GAINE's *N. Y. Gazette &
Mercury, September* 28, 1776.

[3] Doctor Peter Tappan was a brother-in-law of General Clinton, the latter
having married Mifs Cornelia Tappan, of Kingfton.

NEW YORK LOYALISTS.

[The following Addreſs to Admiral and General Howe, on the occaſion of their ſucceſſful occupation of the city of New York in 1776, is an intereſting ſpecimen of that claſs of papers which is ſtill ſo popular among the ſubjects of European rulers, and eſpecially ſo ſince it conveys to us the ſentiments of the loyal inhabitants of "Old New York," their numbers, and their names.

An examination of theſe names has ſhown us the character of thoſe who adhered to the fortunes of the crown, in a ſtronger light than any ſimilar paper now extant; and while the names of the few wealthy landed gentry and thoſe of the clergy head the liſt, it will be ſeen that the petty officers in the cuſtom-houſe and poſt-office, the Faculty of the college, and even the unlicenſed keepers of pot-houſes in the vicinity of the markets, were alſo impreſſed into the queſtionable ſervice of adding their names—under the dread, it may be, of loſing their ſituations or incurring proſecutions as a penalty of their refuſal.

The names of ſome few well-known citizens will be found in the liſt; the greater portion, however, are thoſe whoſe bearers, even at this early date, have paſſed away and been entirely forgotten.]

To the Right Honorable, Richard, Lord Viſcount Howe
—of the Kingdom of Ireland—

And to His Excellency the Honorable William Howe
Eſqr General of his Majeſty's Forces in America: the
King's Commiſſioners for reſtoring Peace to his Majeſtys
Colonies in North America——

Your Excellencies, by your declaration, bearing date
July 14th, 1776, having ſignified, that "the King is deſir-
" ous to deliver his American Subjects from the Calamities

" of War and other Oppreffions which they now undergo;
" and to reftore the Colonies to his protection and peace "—
and by a fubfequent Declaration, dated Sepr. 19th 1776,
having alfo been pleafed to exprefs your defire " to Confer
" with his Majefty's well affected fubjects, upon the means
" of reftoring the public Tranquility and eftablifhing a per-
" manent union with every Colony, as a part of the Britifh
Empire.—We Therefore, whofe names are hereunto Sub-
fcribed, Inhabitants of the City and County of New York,
in the province of New York, reflecting with the tendereft
emotions of Gratitude on this Inftance of his Majefty's
paternal Goodnefs; and encouraged by the Affectionate
manner in which his Majeftys gracious purpofe hath been
conveyed to us by your Excellencies, who have thereby
evinced that Humanity, is infeperable from that true Mag-
nanimity and thofe enlarged fentiments which form the
moft Shining Characters—beg leave to reprefent to your
Excellencies—

That we bear true allegiance to our Rightful Sovereign
George the Third as well as warm affection to his facred
perfon Crown and Dignity.—That we Efteem the conftitutional Supremacy of Great Britain, over thefe Colonies, and
other depending parts of his Majeftys dominions, as Effential to the Union, Security, and Welfare, of the whole
Empire, and fincerely lament the Interruption of that Har-
mony, which formerly fubfifted between the Parent State
and thefe her Colonies—That many of the Loyal Citizens

have been driven away by the Calamities of War and the Spirit of Perfecution which lately prevailed; or fent to New England, and other diftant Parts We therefore hoping that the fufferings which our abfent fellow citizens undergo for their Attachment to the Royal Caufe may plead in their behalf; humbly pray that Your Excellencies would be pleafed on thefe our dutiful reprefentations to Reftore this City & County to his Majefty's Protection and Peace——

New York Octr 16th—1776

LIST OF SIGNERS.[1]

Haob Aaron, John Abeel, Abm. J. Abramfe, Philip Ackert,[2] Jeramiah Ackley, John Ackley, Abraham Adams, Edward Agar, Ernelt Aimes, Jeronimus Akemfen, Stephen Allen, Thomas Allen, George Alliew, Robert Allifon, Jeronemus Alltyne, John Alltyne, James Amar, John Amer-

[1] In the following alphabetical arrangement of the names, their original order has been departed from for the fake of affording more ready reference, and to avoid the neceffity of too tedious an index. Where the fame name was found more than once, it has been indicated by a figure follow'ng it, fhowing the number of times that it appeared in the lift. Whether thefe in all cafes denoted different individuals it is now difficult to determine, but the probability is that they did not in every inftance.

Fuller information concerning fome of thefe figners will be found in a valuable work entitled, "The American Loyalifts; or, Biographical Sketches of Adherents to the Britifh Crown," by Lorenzo Sabine, Efq. 8vo, Bofton, 1847.

[2] Philip Acker, a retailer of liquors in George ftreet, oppofite the Barrack gate.

man, John Amiel, Jun., John Amory, Daniel Amos, John
Anderiefe, Stephen Anderrefe, John Antill,[1] Lewis Antill,
Chas Wd Apthorpe,[2] John Archer, Philip Arcularius, Fran-
cis Arden,[3] Michael Arnott, Peter Arrell, Gilbert Afh, V.
Pierce Afhfield, Robert Atkins, Thomas Atkinfon, Richard
Auchmuty, Robert N. Auchmuty, Samuel Auchmuty,[4] Dan-
iel Aymar (2), William Aymer, William Axtell.[5]

Theophylact Bache, Wm Backhoufe, John Badger, Jo-
seph Bagley, Elias Bailey, William Bailey, Samuel Baldwin,
Wm Balfour, Ifaac Ball, Titus Ball, Evert Banker, Jun.,
Peter Bannot, Paulus Banta, Edward Barden, George
Barke, Thomas Barnes, Henrich Barr, John Barwick, Sam
Bates, William Bauman, Lawe Bayard, Robert Bayard,
Samuel Bayard,[6] Wm Bayard,[7] William Bayley, Thomas

---

[1] John Antill, Efq., poftmafter of the city and agent for the packet-boats.

[2] Charles Ward Apthorpe was a member of the council, refiding at Bloomingdale.

[3] Francis Arden was a butcher doing bufinefs in Fly market—the owner
of Molyneaux the boxer, who was known as " Pete Arden " while he was
in flavery in New York.

[4] Rev. Samuel Auchmuty, D. D., rector of Trinity Church, New York.
He graduated at Harvard Univerfity in 1742; and on the 3d of March,
1777, he died in this city.

[5] Colonel William Axtell was a member of the council, refiding at Flatbufh, L. I.

[6] Samuel Bayard, one of the firm of William Bayard & Co., importers.
He was alfo affiftant fecretary of the province.

[7] Colonel William Bayard, head of the old mercantile houfe of William
Bayard & Co. In the earlier ftages of the Revolutionary ftruggle he acted
with the people, and was a member of the " Committee of Fifty." He alfo
entertained the Maffachufetts delegates at his houfe on the North River, in 1775.

Bean, Jacob Beitturnner, James Bell, Jofeph Bell, Samuel Bell, Jun., William Bell, Grove Bend, John Bengfton, John Bennet, Chriftopher Benfon,[1] Jacob Berger, Henry Bernt, Peter Berton, Fred[k] Bicker, John Binches, Mofes Bingham, John Bifhop, Richard Black, John Blackare, Patrick Blancheville, Ifaac Blanck, Jeremiah Blanck, Waldron Blean,[2] Daniel Blockner, Chriftian Bloom, Archibald Blundell, Chriftopher Blundell, James Board, Henry Boel,[3] Jacob Boelen, Nicholas J. Bogart, Peter Bogart,[4] Chriftian Bollmain, Anthony Bolton, Jacob Bofher, Fred. Botticher, John Bowles, Samuel Bowne, Samuel Boyer, Thomas Braine, David Bramar, Charles John Brannon, Ifaac Brafher, Ifaac Bratt, Simon Brealfed, Elias Brevoort, Henry Brevoort,[5] George Brewerton, Jacob Brewerton, James Brewfter, Alexander Bridges, John Bridgwater,[6] David Brill, John Brooks, Ab[m] Brower, Sebtent Brower, Charles Brown,[7] William Brown, James Browne, John

[1] Chriftopher Benfon, an unlicenfed retailer of liquors, oppofite the theatre, fouth fide of John ftreet, near Broadway.

[2] Waldron Blean was captain in the third battalion of New Jerfey volunteers in 1782.

[3] Henry Boel, "Clerk to the Poft Office."

[4] Peter Bogert, refiding in Dock (now Water) ftreet.

[5] Henry Brevoort, a market gardener in the vicinity of the prefent Fifth avenue and Wafhington fquare. The father of the late Henry Brevoort who refided in that vicinity.

[6] John Bridgewater, an unlicenfed retailer of liquors "near the new Dutch Church" (corner of Fulton and William ftreets).

[7] Charles Brown, an unlicenfed retailer of liquors, on the corner of Broad ftreet and Verlattenberg hill (Exchange place, west from Broad ftreet).

16

Browne, Thomas Brownejohn,[1] Jofeph Browning, Robert
Brunfon, James Bryad, Thomas Buchanan,[2] Andries Buhler,
William Will[m] Bull, Olive Burgefs, John Burns, Thomas
Buroton, John Burrowe, Wm Burton, Charles Bufh, James
Bufh, John Buxton, Godfrey Bydebuck, Garrard Byrn.

John Calder, William Caldwell, Samuel Camfield, Daniel
Campbell,[3] D. Campbell, Duncan Campbell,[4] George Camp-
bell, John Campbell (2), Jofiah Cannon, Dennis Carleton,
Adam Carr, Anthony Carr, Robert Carr, Gideon Carltang,
Thomas Carter, Thomas Cater, Richard Cayhterry, Tadmas
Chadwick, Jn[o] Chapman, Robert Cheefeman,[5] Jofeph
Chew, Johannis Chorberker, Alexander Clark,[6] Archibald
Clark, Daniel Clark, John Clark,[7] Clement Cooke Clarke,
John Clarke, Scott L. Clark, Samuel Clayton, Thomas
Cleathen, William Clofworthy, William Cochran, Philip

[1] Thomas Brownejohn, a druggift and apothecary, doing bufinefs at the
corner of Wall ftreet and Hanover fquare (*now Pearl ftreet*), next door to
the book ftore of Hugh Gaine.

[2] Thomas Buchanan, one of the celebrated firm of Walter and Thomas
Buchanan, importers and fhipping merchants. This houfe was rendered
unufually confpicuous from the fact that to it was configned the tea-fhip
which was returned to London, with its cargo, by the people of New York,
in April, 1774.

[3] Daniel Campbell, a retailer of liquors at Corlies Hook.

[4] Duncan Campbell, an unlicenfed retailer of liquors in Beekman ftreet,
near St. George's Chapel.

[5] Robert Cheefeman, a retailer of liquors in Broadway, near Pearl ftreet.

[6] Alexander Clark, a retailer of liquors in New Chappel ftreet (*now Wyf
Broadway*).

[7] John Clark (or Clarke?). If the former, during thirty years the clerk
of Trinity Church, who, in June, 1783, removed to St. John, New Brunf-

Cockrem, Wm. Cockroft,[1] Joseph Coff, James Coggeshall,[2] Aaron Cohn, Charles Colbourn, John Cole, Joseph Collines, Thomas Collister, Mathias Compton, Nicholas Connery, John Cooder, George Cook, William Cook, John Clarke Cooke, Michael Coon, Henry Coons, William Corbey, James Corin, George Corselius, William Corselius, Andrew Couglan, Conrad Coun, Francis Cowley, John Cox, Ludwig Cox, Bartholemeu Coxetter, Dennis Coyl, Patrick Coyle, Peter Covenhoven, Robert Crannell, John Crawford, John Crawley, Belthar Creamer, Lud. Creamer, Martin Creiger,[3] George Croger, John Ludtz Croufcoup, Pictor Crowder, Jno Harris Cruger,[4] William Cullen, George Cummings, Matthew Cushing.

Benjamin Daffigney, John Damlong, John Darg, Jno Baltis Dash, Sen.,[5] John B. Dash, Jun., John Davan,[6] John

wick, and in August, 1846, still lived there. If the latter, a retailer of liquors in Robinson street.

[1] William Cockroft, an old merchant who had long been a dealer in "European and India" goods, near the Fly Market.

[2] James Coggeshall, "Land Waiter," attached to the custom-house in the port.

[3] Martin Cregier, a retailer of liquors in Nassau street.

[4] John Harris Cruger, son-in-law of General Oliver De Lancey. He was treasurer of the city; a member of the council; a lieutenant-colonel in the service, commanding at Fort Ninety-six when it was attacked in 1781; and, at the peace, retired to England.

[5] John Baltis Dash, senior, kept a hardware and tin store opposite the Oswego, or Broadway Market.

[6] John Davan, leather dresser and breeches maker, at the sign of the "Crown and Breeches," next door to Messrs. Robert and John Murray, Queen (*now* *Pearl*) street, near the Fly Market, where he transacted a very extensive wholesale and retail trade.

Davan, Jun., James Davis, Wm. Day,[1] William Deall,
James Dean, Elk. Deane, James Deas,[2] Jno. De Clue, John
De Foreſt, Joſeph Degroot, Sen., Iſaac De Lamate, John
Delancey,[3] Jno De Lancey, Jun., Oliver Delancy,[4] Jona-
than Delano, Francis Humbert De la Roche, James De-
masney, Michael Denny, Elias Deſbroſſes, James Deſbroſſes,[5]
James Deſbroſſes, Jun., Henry Detloff, John Detrich, Will[m]
Devereaux, David Devoore,[6] Guert Sp[t] De Wint, John
Dikeman,[7] Barnnae Dill, Silvanus Dillingham, Anthony
Dodane, Amos Dodge, Thomas Dodge, Adam Dolmidge,
Robert Donkirz, Archibald Donnaldſon, Thomas Dor-
man, Peter Dorry, Walter Dougall, John Dougan, Ed-
ward Doughty,[8] Matthew Douglaſs,[9] John Dowers, James

---

[1] William Day, a retailer of liquors in Warren ſtreet. At the cloſe of the
war he removed to St. John, New Brunſwick, and was one of the original
grantees of that city.

[2] James Deas, a perukemaker and hairdreſſer, reſiding in the lower part of
Broad ſtreet.

[3] John De Lancey, ſon of Peter De Lancey, of Weſtcheſter county, and
his ſucceſſor in the General Aſſembly as repreſentative of the borough of
Weſtcheſter, which office he retained until 1775, when he was elected a member of the Provincial Congreſs.

[4] Oliver De Lancey was a brigadier-general in the Britiſh ſervice, and died
in Beverly, Yorkſhire, England, in 1785, aged ſixty-eight years.

[5] James Deſbroſſes, doing buſineſs "at the Ship-yards," in the vicinity of
Catharine ſtreet, Eaſt River.

[6] David Devoore had been a miller doing buſineſs near the Kiſſing Bridge,
which ſpanned "Devoore's mill-ſtream." He is ſaid to have built "Cato's"
hotel.

[7] John Dickeman, alderman of the Out Ward of the city.

[8] Edward Doughty, an unlicenſed liquor dealer on Whitehall Dock.

[9] Matthew Douglaſs, one of the firm of Douglaſs and Van Tuyl, unlicenſed

Downes, John Drummond, Edward Drury, Cornelius Dru-yer, John Dudley, Chriſtopher Dugan, Robely Dukely, Nicholas Duley, Jacob Dulmadge, John Duly, John Du-mont, Joſeph Durbunow, Jacob Durje, Derick Duryee.

William Eames, Edward Eaſtman, Daniel Ebbets, Chriſtian Eggert, Samuel Ellis (2), William Elliſon, Francis Elſworth, Benjⁿ Engliſh, James Ettridge.

George Fach, Alexʳ Fairlie, Samuel Falkenhau, Edmund Fanning,[1] John Faulkner, David Fenton, Robert Fenton, Dennis Ferguſon, Duncan Ferguſon, James Ferguſon, Jnᵒ Adam Finch (2), Walter Fitz Gerald, John Fleming (3), James Fletcher, Michael Flim, James Flynn, George Folliot,[2] Alexʳ Forbes, Robert Fordham, Daniel Forſchee, Henry Forſter, John Forſyth, Alexander Fortune, William For-

dealers in liquors at retail on the corner oppoſite the Fly Market (*foot of Maiden Lane*).

[1] Colonel Edmund Fanning, ſecretary and ſon-in-law of Governor William Tryon. He was originally from North Carolina, where he was exceedingly unpopular; and it is probable that Tryon's adminiſtration of that government was ſeriouſly impa red from that cauſe. In 1777, he raiſed a corps of loy-aliſts, which was called the "Aſſociated Refugees," and ſometimes "The King's American Regiment," of which he had the command; and it was ſomewhat celebrated in the Southern campaigns of 1780-1, for its ſpirited conduct in the field. At the cloſe of the war he retired to Nova Scotia, where he became lieutenant-governor; and, in 1786, he was tranſferred, in the ſame capacity, to Prince Edward's Iſland, where he remained until 1805. The time of his death is not recorded.

[2] George Folliot was a merchant tranſacting an extenſive buſineſs in this city. He was elected a member of the Provincial Congreſs, in 1775, but declined; and he alſo declined to ſerve as a member of the "Committee of One Hundred," to which he had been elected.

tune, George Fowler, John Fowler,[1] Samuel Franklin, Walter Franklin, Lovis Frauzers, Alexander Frafer, Walter Frazer, Ab^m Fruge, Daniel Fueter, David Fuhrle, Michael Fung.

Chriftian Gabble, Alex^r Galbreath, John Gallaudett, David Ganner, Francis Gantz, Peter Garrabrance, Jun., Frederick Bonn Garten, Matthew Gafkin, Archibald Gatfield,[2] Benjamin Gatfield, Nicholaus Gaub, Andrew Gautier,[3] David Geler, Francois Gerard, William Gifting, Leonard Gildert, Thomas Gillefpie, Richard Glebets, John Glover, William Goddington, Ab^m Gomez, Mofes Gomez, Jun., Peter Goodman, Lodwig Gounzer, Abraham Gouvernuer, James Govers, Peter Graff, Edward Grant, John Grant (2), Thomas Graves, Andrew Gray, John Gray, Wm. Gray, David Gregg,[4] Iean George Greffand, John Grierfon, Robert Griffith, John Griffiths,[5] John Grigg,[6] Thomas Grigg, D. Grim,[7] Jacob Grim, Peter Grim, Charles Grimfley, Jacob Grindlemyer, Thomas Grifdall, Hendrick Gulick.

[1] John Fowler, refiding at "Little Bloomingdale."

[2] Archibald Gatfield, an unlicenfed dealer of liquors in Slaughter-houfe ftreet.

[3] Andrew Gautier, alderman of the Dock Ward.

[4] David Gregg, probably one of the celebrated firm of Gregg, Cunningham & Co., merchants tranfacting a very heavy bufinefs with foreign countries.

[5] John Griffiths, "Mafter of the Port."

[6] John Grigg, a retailer of liquors in Sloat alley. At a fubfequent period he appears to have become a tallow-chandler, tanner, etc., in which bufinefs he became infolvent in 1783.

[7] David Grim, the antiquarian tavern keeper, fo well known and gratefully remembered in New York by every ftudent of *local* hiftory. He formerly

Frederick Haas. George Haaßis. Mathias Haerlman. John Halden, Edward Hall. Henry Hall. Peter Hall.[1] James Hallet, Samuel Hallet. Daniel Halfted. John Hamilton[2] (2), Joseph Handforth. Ab[m] Hangworth, William Hanna. Goft. Hans, Mecil Hanfen, Martin Hanfhee. Johannes Harbell. John Hardenburgh,[3] David Hardley, Laurance Hardman. John Harris, Richard Harris (2). Thomas Harrifon, Charles Hart. George Hartman. Laurance Hartwick. Charles Haus. Thomas Hautzman. William Hauxhurft.[4] Joseph Haviland. William Hay. Barrak Hays. David Hays. Thomas Haywood, Jacob Heartz. Geo. Heath. Fred. Wm. Hecht,[5] Ifaac Hedges. Valten Hefner. Andrew Heifter. John Henderfon. Uriah Hendricks. William Hervey. John Jacob Hetzell. James Hewett. Garrit Heyer. Daniel Hick. Whitehead Hicks.[6] Thomas Hiett. Joseph Hildrith, John Hillman. Michael Hillfteam. John Hilyer. Joseph Hitchcock. Johannis Hoffman. Michael Hoffman.

kept "the Three Tuns," in Chapel ftreet; but, in 1776, he was a retailer in William ftreet.

[1] Peter Hall, a retailer of liquors in Peck flip.

[2] John Hamilton, agent, probably a refugee from South Carolina, who had accepted military appointment under the crown. *Vide* Butler's ftatement, Tomlinfon MSS.

[3] John Hardenbrook, affiftant alderman of the Out Ward of the city.

[4] William Hawxhurft, a merchant dealing in pig-iron, anchors, pot-afh, kettles, negro-wenches and children, horfes, etc.

[5] Fred. Wm. Hecht, a German, refiding in Queen (*now Pearl*) ftreet, who had been commiffioned by Governor Tryon as a captain in the loyalift fervice, as early as October, 1776.

[6] Whitehead Hicks, mayor of the city of New York, from 1766 to 1776.

James Holden,[1] Peter Holmes, James Hope, Rinier Hopper, Yallefs Hopper, Thomas Hopwood, Robert Horne, James Horner,[2] Thomas Horffield, Daniel Horfmanden,[3] Jacob Hortz, Alexander Hofack,[4] Bernard Mich[l] Houfeal,[5] Robert Howard, James Hoy, George Hubnors, Benjamin Hugget,[6] Richard Hughes, Thomas Hughes, Robert Hull,[7] Jofeph Hunt, John Fred Huntill, Diederick Hyer.

James Imbrie, Charles Inglis,[8] Levy Ifrael.

Daniel Jacobs, John Johnfon, Robert Johnfton,[9] David Jones, John Jones[10] (2), Samuel Jones, William Jones.

Chriftian Kauff, John Keen, Andrew Keer, John Kenne-

[1] John Holden, a retailer of liquors near the Upper Barracks, in the upper part of the Park.

[2] James Horner, an unlicenfed retailer of liquors in French-church (*now* *Pine*) ftreet, near Broadway.

[3] Daniel Horfmanden was the chief juftice of the colony. His wife was Mary, daughter of Colonel Abraham De Peyfter, and widow of Rev. Mr. Vefey, rector of Trinity Church, New York; and he died at Flatbufh, Long Ifland, September 23d, 1778, aged eighty-eight years.

[4] Alexander Hofack, an unlicenfed retailer of liquors in Dey ftreet.

[5] Rev. Bernard Michael Houfeall, V. D. M., fenior paftor of the Lutheran German Church.

[6] Benjamin Huggett, a grocer and dealer in liquors, and affiftant alderman of the North Ward, living and doing bufinefs on the corner of Naffau and Fair (*now Fulton*) ftreet.

[7] Robert Hull, at "Hull's Tavern," No. 18 Broadway.

[8] Rev. Charles Inglis, affiftant rector of Trinity Church, New York. He fucceeded Rev. Dr. Auchmuty, as rector; but, in 1783, he was obliged to refign and take refuge in Nova Scotia, and fubfequently, he was appointed Lord Bifhop of that colony. In 1809, he was a member of the Council of the Province; and he died in 1816, aged eighty-two.

[9] Robert Johnfon, an unlicenfed retailer of liquors, in Ferry ftreet.

[10] John Jones, M. D., profeffor of furgery in King's (*Columbia*) College.

dy, Jnº J. Kempe.[1] Johannis Kefer, Aaron Keyfer, Stephen Kibble, James Killmafter, Linus King, John Kingfton, Jofeph Kirby, Benjⁿ Kiffam,[2] Philip Kiflick,[3] George Klein, John Klein,[4] Jacob Klinck, John C. Knapp,[5] Jacob Kneht, Abᵐ Knickerbacker, John Knoblock, Robert Knox.

Joft Lachman, Nicholas Lackman, William La Croix, Stephen Ladlam, John Lagear, Thomas Lahriwick, Thomas Lamb, Albert Lamkin, Henry Law, John Lawrance, Stephen Leach, James Leadbelter, John Leake, John Legar, Jofeph Lee, John Lell, Garret Lent, James Leonard, Robert Leonard, Alexander Leflie,[6] James Lefly, Michael Leffler, David Levifon, Chriftopher Leviffen, John Lewis (2), Patrick Leyburn, Daniel Lightfoot, Barnard Lin, Charles Lindaman, Stroud Cotton Lincoln, Johannis Lindner, Philip

---

[1] John Tabor Kempe was the attorney-general of the province.

[2] Benjamin Kiffam, a leading lawyer in the city of New York, under whom Lindley Murray, the grammarian, and John Jay, the chief juftice of the United States, read law.

[3] Philip Kiflick, vintner and diftiller, at the upper end of Great Queen ftreet (*now Pearl ftreet*), where his ftock of "Home-fpun Brandy and Gin, very little inferior to French Brandy and Holland Gin," together with an extenfive affortment of wines, liquors, porter, and cider, were offered for fale.

[4] John Klyne, a baker, who at that time lodged with Mr. Daniel Mefnard, Duke (*now Stone*) ftreet.

[5] John Cogghill Knapp, a notorious pettifogger—a convict who had fled from England for his own benefit—who was doing bufinefs on the corner of Broad ftreet and Verlattenberg Hill.

[6] Alexander Leflie, A. M., head mafter of the grammar-fchool of King's (*Columbia*) College. There was, alfo, an Alexander Leflie, who was an unlicenfed retailer of liquors, near the Barracks (*Park*) in Chatham ftreet.

17

Linzie, Leonard Lifpenard, William Litch, George Little,
John Lockhart, John Lockman, John Logan, Chriftopher
Long, James Long, John Long, Charles Lorrilliard, Lam-
bert Losije, William Loughead, James Love, William
Lowndes, Thomas Lowrey,[1] William Lowrie, John Andries
Lucaim, Henry Ludlam, Daniel Ludlow, Geo. D. Ludlow,[2]
Thomas Grey Luebe, Thomas Lupton, Philip Lydig,
Thomas Lynch.[3]

W[m] M[c]Bride,[4] James M[c]Candefs, Thomas M[c]Carty, Ed-
ward M[c]Collom, Patrick M[c]Connegall, John M[c]Cormick,
Archibald M[c]Donald,[5] John M[c]Donnald, Benjamin M[c]Dow-
al, Hugh M[c]Dowll, Charles M[c]Evers, John M[c]Fall, Dou-
gall M[c]Farlane, John M[c]Gillaray, Hugh M[c]Intire, Patrick
M[c]Kay, John M[c]Kenzie, John M[c]Kinlay, Peter M[c]Lean,
Neil M[c]Leod, John M[c]Manomy, William M[c]Nabb, Daniel
M[c]Onnully, Donald M[c]Pherfon, Dougald M[c]Pherfon, John

---

[1] Thomas Lowry, an unlicenfed retailer of liquors, oppofite Ofwego market, in Broadway.

[2] George Duncan Ludlow was one of the juftices of the Supreme Court of
the Province. He refided at Hempftead, Long Ifland, and fuffered greatly
from the incurfions of the Americans. In 1780, he was appointed mafter of
the rolls, and fuperintendent of the police on Long Ifland; and having taken
refuge in New Brunfwick, in 1783, he was a member of the firft council in
that province. As the fenior member of that body, he adminiftered the government, *ad interim*; and he was the firft chief juftice of the Supreme Court
of that colony. He died at Fredericton, February 12, 1808.

[3] Thomas Lynch, a dealer in liquors and negroes, in Duke (*now Stone*) ftreet.

[4] William McBride, an unlicenfed retailer of liquors, in Cooper's ftreet,
near Lupton's Wharf.

[5] Archibald McDonald, a licenfed retailer of liquors, in Church ftreet.

McPherſon,[1] Thomas McWilliams, John Machet, Peter Machet, John Maffet, Thomas Mahan, Abraham Malunar, Peter Mange, Moſes Marden,[2] Jones Marle, Joakim Marr, John Marſhall[3] (2), Nathaniel Marlton, Henry Marx, John Maſkelyn, Thomas Maſon,[4] Matthew Maugere, James Maxwell, Thomas Medanel, John Michalſal, John Middlemaſs, Peter Middleton,[5] James Mildrum,[6] David Henry Millar, Charles Miller, Hugh Miller, Jacob Miller, John Miller, Joſhua Miller, Michael Miller, Philip Miller, Robert Miller, Thomas Miller, Saml Millſon, John Minuſs, James Mitchell, Viner Mitchell, Jacob Moell, William Mook, Joſeph Moon, Abm Moor, Bluſty Moor, John Moor, Benjn Moore,[7] Boltis Moore, Henry Moore, James Moore, Jeremiah Moore, John Moore[8] (2), James Moran,[9] Philip Morgan, George Morrel, Martin Morris, Charles Morie,

[1] John McPherſon, a retailer of liquors doing buſineſs in Broadway.

[2] Moſes Mardin, an unlicenſed retailer of liquors, in Broadway, oppoſite the Bowling Green.

[3] John Marſhall, an unlicenſed retailer of liquors, in Old Dutch Church ſtreet (*Exchange Pl.*).

[4] Thomas Maſon, a retailer of liquors, in Broadway, corner of Beaver ſtreet.

[5] Dr. Peter Middleton, profeſſor of the theory of medicine and of materia medica in King's (*Columbia*) College. (*Vide* page 72.)

[6] James Maldrem, an unlicenſed retailer of liquors, "oppoſite the Slip Market."

[7] Rev. Benjamin Moore, aſſiſtant rector of Trinity Church, New York, ſucceeded Dr. Inglis, as rector, and ſubſequently became biſhop of the diocefe. He died February 27, 1816.

[8] John Moore, deputy collector of cuſtoms at this port.

[9] James Moran was firſt clerk in the cuſtom-houſe in this city.

Ifaac Mott, William Mucklevain, Jeremiah Mullar, Charles Muller, Frederick Muller, George Muller, John God. Muller, Samuel Murgiffroyd, Philip Murphy, Lindley Murray, John Murray, Jun., Robert Murray,[1] George Myer, James Myer, Samuel Myers, George Myir.

Michael Nailor, Samuel Naroy, David Nathan, David Navaro, James Neaven, Cafpar Neftle, Samuel Nichols, Edward Nicoll, William Niers, John Nixon, John Noblit, William Norman, Benj[n] Norwood, John Norwood, Vanderclife Norwood, Valentine Nutter.[2]

Garret Oaks,[3] Henry O Brien, Benj[n] Ogden, John Ogilvie, Alexander Ogfbury, John O Neill, Jofeph Orchard, Philip Ofward, Jacob Ott, Jofeph Owl, Walter Owl.

Aaron Packman, William Pagan, Hayes Pannell, Francis Panton, William Parcells, Thomas Parrifien, John Pafca, William Patton, Thomas Paul, James O Pava, George Peitfch, Gibbert Pell, Richard Penny, Henry W. Perry, Mervin Perry,[4] Harry Peters, Hugh Philips, Adolph. Philipfe, Fred[k] Philipfe, William Poole, James Potter, Jacob

---

[1] Robert Murray, a Friend, and head of the houfe of Murray, Sanfom & Co., among the leading merchants of Colonial New York. His place of bufinefs was in Queen (*Pearl*) ftreet, between Beckman and Burling Slips; and his refidence on Murray Hill. (*Vide* page 29.)

[2] Valentine Nutter, bookfeller and ftationer, oppofite the coffee-houfe in Wall ftreet, where he remained until the clofe of the war.

[3] Garret Oaks, a retailer of liquors doing bufinefs on Cruger's Wharf, (*between Old and Coenties Slips*).

[4] Mervin Perry, "Repeating and Plain Watch and Clock maker, from London," at the fign of "the Dial," fix doors below Gaine's printing office, the fame fide the way (*Pearl ftreet*, eight doors below Wall ftreet).

Pozer,[1] Thomas Price, David Provooft, David Provolt, Capper Pryer, Edward Pryor, John Philip Puntzius.

Benjamin Quackenbofs, Luke C. Quick, Thomas Quill.

John Randiker, Rem. Rapelje,[2] John Rapp, Frederick Ranfier, Henry Reden, Stephen Reeves,[3] George Reieble, Nich⁵ Remind, George Remfen,[4] John A. Remfen, Jacob Refler, Fred^k Rhinelander,[5] Philip Rhinelander, Henry Ricker, David Rider, John Rifler, John Ritter, J. Roberts,[6] John Robertfon, Ezekiel Robins, Jarvis Roebuck, James Rogers,[7] Godfred Roltonour, Cornelius Romme, Alexander Rofs (2), James Rofs, Robert Rofs, Jafper Ruckell, William Ruddle, Fred^k Ruger, Jacob Ruoifer, Cornelius Ryan, John Rykeman.

John Sackett, John Samler, Thomas Sample, Sam. Samuel, Jacob Sanfar, John Saunders, Nicholas Scande, John Scandlin, Coenradt Schultez, Chriftian Schultz, Adam

[1] Jacob Pozer, proprietor of "The Philadelphia Stage houfe," in White Hall.

[2] Rem Rapelje, whofe punifhment inflicted by the people on the twelfth of June, 1776, has been defcribed in Peter Elting's letter to Captain Varick, page 97.

[3] Stephen Reeves, formerly one of the firm of Whitehoufe & Reeve, jewellers, doing bufinefs in Queen (*Pearl*) ftreet, near the corner of Barling Slip.

[4] George Remfen, an unlicenfed retailer of liquors, in Water ftreet, near the Exchange Bridge (*Broad ftreet*).

[5] Frederic Rhinelander, a very heavy importer of crockery and other merchandise, who tranfacted bufinefs at Burling Slip; and in 1783, tranfacted bufinefs at No. 168 Water ftreet.

[6] John Roberts, Efqr., high fheriff of the city and county of New York.

[7] James Rogers, an unlicenfed retailer of liquors, in Queen (*Pearl*) ftreet.

Schuumburg,[1] Thos Scorfield,[2] William Scott,[3] J. Seagroove, Joſhua Seaman, James Seamans, Levy Seamans, Caſper Semler, Jacob Shafer, George Shaw, James Shaw, John Shaw,[4] John Sheppherd, Jun., E. G. Shewkirk, Daniel Shier, Henry Shier, Martin Shier, John Shoals, Abraham Shotwell, John Shouldis, Chriſtopher Shundel, Richd Sibley, Henry Simmerman, Joſeph Simmons, George Simpſon, Saml Sp. Skinner, John Slidell, Joſhua Slidell, John Sloan, John Smart, Walter Smealee, George Smelzell, Albert Smith, Barnardus Smith, Chriſtopher Smith, Johannis Smith, John Smith,[5] Jno Sam. Smith, Richd Smith, Robert Smith, Thomas Smith,[6] William Smith (3), John Snell,[7] Randolph Snowden, Henry Sobouvon, Iſaac Solomons, Tiunis Somerindicke, Peter Sparling, William Spenns, John Spers, Hugh Spier, John Spier, Frederick Spirck, Gregory Springall, Hugh Sproat, Thomas Sproat, Jacob Spury, Melcher Stahl, Daniel Stallmann, George Stanton, Michael Stavener, John Steel, Robert Steel, Wm. Stepple,

[1] Adam Shamburg, an unlicenſed dealer in liquors, in Chatham ſtreet.

[2] Thomas Scorfield, a licenſed retailer of liquors, "back of Henry White's."

[3] William Scott, a deputy ſheriff of the county of New York. He was a retailer of liquors on Broadway, near the Ofwego market.

[4] John Shaw, a jeweller doing buſineſs at the ſign of "the Crown," in Naſſau ſtreet, near John ſtreet.

[5] John Smith, a warden of the port.

[6] Thomas Smith, a merchant doing buſineſs in Hanover ſquare.

[7] John Snell, an unlicenſed retailer of liquors, oppoſite the ſhip-yards, in the vicinity of our Market ſtreet.

James Stevenfon, George Stewart,[1] Jofeph Steyner, John
Stiles, Thomas Stilwell, Jan. Stockholm, Nicholas Stonpf,
Philip Stoneftreet, Benjamin Stout,[2] Benjamin Stout, Jun.,
John B. Stout, Richard Stout, Robert Stout, James Striker,
Jofeph Stringhans, Johannis Stroutter, James Stuart, Fran-
cis Stuck, P. Stuyvefant, Caleb Sutton, William Sutton,
Godfred Swan, Willm Swanfir, Chriftopher Sweedland,
John Swere, Philip Sykes.

William Tailer, James Taylor, Willet Taylor, William
Taylor, David Thomas, Henry Thomas, Walter Thomas,
David Thompfon, George Thompfon, John Thompfon (2),
Peter Thompfon, Saml Thopfon, Fred. Thonnaird, Albertus
Tiebout, Robert Till, James Toffie, William Tongue,[3] Daniel
Tooker, Silas Totten, George Trail, Jonathan Treemain,
Francis Trevillian,[4] Tobias Trim, James Tucker, Jonathan
Twene, Jacob Tyler.

Harman Utt, Benjn Underhill, Nicodemus Ungerar,
John Chriftopher Urmhaulter, George Urlt, Henry Uftick,[5]
Wm Uftick.

[1] James Stewart, a dealer in dry goods, oppofite Frederic Rhinelander's, in
Burling Slip.

[2] Benjamin Stout, a wholefale dealer in wines, groceries, dye-woods, etc.,
doing bufinefs in Queen (*Pearl*) ftreet, near Peck Slip.

[3] William Tongue, a general broker and auctioneer, doing bufinefs oppofite
to Hugh Gaine's bookftore, Hanover fquare, next door but one from Wall
ftreet.

[4] Francis Traveller (*Trevillian*), an unlicenfed liquor dealer in Murray
ftreet.

[5] Henry Uftick, one of the firm of William and Henry Uftick, importers,
etc., whofe infidelity to the non-importation agreement had excited the in-

Fauconier Vallean, John Vance, Augt Van Cortlandt,
Corn^s V. D. Bergh, Mindert Van Every, Jacobus Van Nor-
dan,^{1} Jacobus Van Norden, Jun., Andrew Van Tuyl, John
Van Vorft, Wynandt Van Zandt,^{2} Thomas Vardill,^{3}
Thomas Vaffie, William Vermilye, Philip Verner.

Wm Waddell,^{4} Ab^m Wagg, John Wagna, George
Walf, John Walker^5 (2), George Wall, John Walmfley, Ja-
cob Walton,^{6} Thomas Warner,^{7} William Waterman, Jacob
Watfon^8 (2), John Watts, James Wear, William Weaver,
Jun., James Webb, William Webb, Arnold Webbers,
Jacob Webbers, Philip Webbers, Michael Weber, Edward
Webfter, Johannis Weifs, James Wells, Oliver Wells,

dignation of the Sons of Liberty, April 6, 1775. Henry was alfo the proprietor of a retail liquor ftore on Potbaker's Hill (*Liberty, near Naffau*).

^{1} Jacob Van Orden, a licenfed retailer of liquors, oppofite the Bear (*Wafh-ington*) Market.

^{2} Wynandt Van Zandt, one of the firm of Van Zandts and Keteltas, importers.

^{3} Thomas Vardell, a warden of the port.

^{4} William Waddell, alderman of the North Ward, refiding in King (*Pine*)
ftreet.

^{5} John Walker, a licenfed retailer of liquors, near the Breaftwork, in the
lower part of Broadway.

^{6} Jacob Walton, one of the firm of William and Jacob Walton & Co.,
importers. He was a member of the General Affembly from this city; and
one of the moft influential citizens of his day. His wife, a daughter of Hon.
Henry Cruger, died on the 1ft Auguft, 1782; and eleven days after, he followed her.

^{7} Thomas Warner, an unlicenfed retailer of liquors at Leary Slip, near the
Ferry ftairs.

^{8} Jacob Watfon, a merchant dealing in pig-iron, anchors, pot-afh kettles,
negro wenches and children, horfes, etc.

George Welſh, Thomas Welſh,[1] Chriſtian Wernir, Evert Weſſels, Gilbert Weſſells,[2] Jno. Wetherhead,[3] Thomas Whaley, Charles White, Henry White,[4] Robert White, Thomas White,[5] William White, John Whitman, George Wighton, Thomas Wilkes, Jacob Wilkins,[6] Robert Wilkinſon, John Michael Will, Abraham Willet, George William, Benjamin Williams, William Williams,[7] George Willis, Jun., Fredk Windiſh, George Winfield, William Winterton, Jno Witterhorn, George Wittmer, John Witzell, John Woods, William Wragg, Thomas Wright, George Wyley.

Abm Young, Hamilton Young,[8] John Young.[9]

George Zindall, Lodwick [?].

[1] Thomas Welſh, a licenſed retailer of liquors, oppoſite the Fly Market.

[2] Gilbert Weſſels, a reſident of Pearl ſtreet.

[3] John Wetherhead was an importer, tranſacting a heavy buſineſs in King ſtreet. He offered the uſual great variety of goods which the merchants of that day kept on hand.

[4] Henry White was a member of the Council. He was a merchant in 1769, doing buſineſs in the De Peyſter houſe, on the Fly; and his advertiſements, offering for ſale the uſual variety of nails, teas, window glaſs, ſail cloth, oſnaburgs, Madeira wine, etc., appear in the papers of that day. He retired to England in 1783.

[5] Thomas White, an unlicenſed retailer of liquors in the Bowery lane.

[6] Jacob Wilkins, a dealer in hardware, bellows, lamp oil, etc., doing buſineſs near Coenties Market.

[7] William Williams, a licenſed retailer of liquors in the Bowery lane.

[8] Hamilton Young, dealer in crockery, dry goods, pork, gold and ſilver buttons, etc., in Little Dock (*Water*) ſtreet, between the Coffee-houſe (*Wall ſtreet*) and Old Slip.

[9] John Young, a wholeſale dealer in groceries, ſilks, etc., doing buſineſs in Smith (*William*) ſtreet.

18

We William Waddell, one of the Alderman of the City & County of New York, Efq^r. and James Downes of the faid City, Gentlemen, Do hereby certify that we attended, the figning of the foregoing Reprefentation, & that the Subfcribers hereunto attended Voluntarily, as Witnefs our hands, this 24th day of October, One Thoufand, feven hundred, & feventy fix,

WILLIAM WADDELL
JAMES DOWNES

ADDRESS TO GOVERNOR TRYON.

To His Excellency Wm Tryon Efq^r, Captain General and Governor in Chief in, and over, the province of New York, and the territories depending thereon in America Chancellor & Vice Admiral of the Same———

We the Inhabitants of the City & County of New York, beg leave to Congratulate your Excellency on your return to the Capital of your Government: and to affure you, that we feel the fincereft Joy on this happy Event, which opens a Profpect that we fhall once more experience the Bleffings of Peace and Security under his Majeftys aufpicious Government & Protection—bleffings which we formerly enjoyed under your Excellency's mild Adminiftration, and which we Ardently wifh to have renewed.———

Perfevering in our Loyalty and Unfhaken attachment to our Gracious Sovereign, in this time of Diftrefs and trial, and anxious to teftify our affection for him, we have embraced the Earliest Opportunity to Petition the Kings Commissioners they would restore this City & County to his Majestys Peace. Although many of the most respectable Citizens, and a much greater number of the Interior Classes, have been driven Off by the Calamities of War, or sent Prisoners to new England, and other distant parts; yet we hope that the numbers still remaining, and who have voluntarily subscribed, may be deemed sufficient to intitle this district to his Majesty's grace—whilst the sufferings which our absent Fellow Citizens undergo for the Royal Cause plead in their behalf with the Commissioners From whose well known humanity, benevolence, and enlarged Sentiments, we have the most flattering Expectations. To your Excellency we naturally look up for Assistance ; we therefore request, that you would be pleased to present our Petition to the Commissioners, and otherwise Exert yourself, that the Prayer of it may be granted : as it is our present desire, and what we Esteem the Greatest earthly Felicity, to remain Subjects of the British Government in union with the Parent State

Signed by Desire, and in behalf of the
Inhabitants by

DANIEL HORSMANDEN

New York Octr 16th, 1776

To which his Excellency was pleased to write the following Letter in answer

New York 25th October—1776.

Sir

    The Address you deliver'd to me in behalf of the Inhabitants of the City & County of New York, cannot fail of being highly agreeable to me, as it was, accompanied, with a dutiful Petition & reprefentation from them to the Kings Commiffioners, for reftoring peace to his Majeftys Colonies—teftifying their Loyalty, to our moft Gracious Sovereign, profeffing a Zealous attachment to the britifh Conftitution, and declaring the warmeft defire, for a lafting union with the parent ftate.

    Still folicitous as I am for the welfare of the Inhabitants of this Colony in General, and earneftly wifhing for a reftoration of Public Harmony, and the re-eftablifhment of the ancient Conftitutional authority of Government, I have cheerfully embraced the Opportunity of prefenting this Day, the Addrefs to Lord Howe, who was pleafed to fignify to me " he would take the earlieft opportunity of com-" municating with General Howe on the Occafion."

    The Inhabitants may be affured I fhall fupport their wifhes with my beft Endeavours, although the Completion of it muft be left to the decifion of his Majeftys Commiffioners, in whom the higheft National confidence is repofed.

        I am with regard

           Sir, your moft Obedient Servant

               WM TRYON.

To the Honble Chief Juftice Horfmanden.

PREPARATIONS FOR EVACUATION.

[The power of the British forces in America having been broken by the capture and defeat of Cornwallis at Yorktown, negotiations were set on foot for bringing about a peace. After the delay of nearly two years, a definitive treaty was signed at Paris by Commissioners appointed for that purpose, and preparations were made for evacuating the city of New York, the last of the British strongholds within the original thirteen states. At the request of Sir Guy Carleton, the British commander-in-chief, three commissioners were appointed by Congress to superintend the embarkations from this port, that no negroes or other property of American inhabitants might be carried away. The commissioners appointed for this purpose were Messrs. Egbert Benson, William S. Smith, and Daniel Parker.

The following letters were written from New York City to General Washington, by Lieutenant-Colonel Smith, while acting in his capacity of commissioner. They will have additional interest when taken in connection with Mr. Butler's "Statement" which follows.]

LIEUTENANT-COLONEL SMITH'S LETTERS.

New York 15th July 1783

Sir

A very confiderable embarkation of Refugees took place laft week bound for Nova Scotia & Canada one large Tranfport was filled with foldiers of different corps for Quebec & a number of the 17th Light Dragoons are difcharged & accompany the Refugees to the new Country —The nonfuch a 64 failed on thurfday laft for Europe with the Regt of Heffe Hannau The infpection of the above veffels compofing a fleet of twenty two fail of Large

Tranſport Ships employ'd me five days in the laſt week.
Mr. Benſon's abſcence and Mr Parkers indiſpoſition throws
the whole weight of Buſineſs upon me, and as they begin
to appear diſpoſed to proceed with vigour upon the buſineſs of the evacuation Mr Benſon's aſſiſtance will be very
acceptable—I ſhall not preſume to make any obſervations
on the advantages which our Country may derive from our
exertions in this Line, as your Excellency is poſſeſſed of a
regular Detail of our proceedings upon the moſt important
Points of our miſſion and the attention which the Britiſh
Commr in Chief has paid to our remonſtrances &c there
fully appear

About two thouſand Heſſians will embark to-morrow &
the next day for Europe—and about one thouſand Blacks
for Nova Scotia, further repreſentations to Sir Guy Carleton upon theſe ſubjects I conceive ſuperfluous & ſhall only
attend to the examination of the ſhips, regiſtering the ſlaves
& ſtopping ſuch Property as is evidently free from the laſt
of their Proclamations Caſes of this kind have preſented
themſelves and I have been ſucceſsful—from the laſt fleet
we brought ſeven blacks but have not been able fully to
deſcide for want of the attendance of the Claimants.

I think it neceſſary to inform your Excellency that ſome
persons from the eaſtern ports of the Continent have forged
in this City a Number of Mr Morris's Notes of the laſt
emmition, the Principals are detected and upon application to the Commandant I obtained a Guard laſt night, had

two of them taken & confined—Sir Guy Carleton is fully difpofed to give every affiftance requifite for their further detection and punifhment

I have the honor to be with great refpect &c

His Excellency Gen¹ Wafhington

NEW YORK 26th Auguft 1733.

Sir

The Books¹ which your Excellency requefted fhould be forwarded by your Letter of the 6ᵗʰ inftant were committed to the Care of Col° Cobb. I fhould have accompanied them with a Letter but was confined to my bed with a fevere fever—from which I have only within a few days recover'd——

The Caps for the Boy's fhould have been forwarded

---

[1] " Soon after the commiffioners arrived in New York, General Wafhington fent to Colonel Smith a lift of the titles of books which he had felected from a catalogue publifhed by a bookfeller in a gazette, and which he requefted Colonel Smith to purchafe for him. The reader may be curious to know the kind of works to which his thoughts were at this time directed. They were the following: Life of Charles the Twelfth; Life of Louis the Fifteenth; Life and Reign of Peter the Great; Robertfon's Hiftory of America; Voltaire's Letters; Vertot's Revolution of Rome and Revolution of Portugal; Life of Guftavus Adolphus; Sully's Memoirs; Goldfmith's Natural Hiftory; Campaigns of Marfhal Turenne; Chambaud's French and Englifh Dictionary; Locke on the Human Underftanding; Robertfon's Charles the Fifth."—Sparks's *Wafhington*, vol. viii., p. 431. To which lift we may add, from a letter of Colonel Smith's, the following works as having been fent by him through Dr. Le Moyer: Moore's Travels, in 5 vols; Young's Journey through Ireland, 2 vols.; and the Trial between Sir Richard Worfley and George Mourin Biffel.

before this had not the workman I employ'd undertook a matter that he was not fufficiently acquainted with   I was obliged to return them to him after they were finifhed & employ another perfon—they fhall be forwarded as foon as they are compleat

Inclofed are two Letters which Came in the laft packett from England

About fix thoufand Heffians have fail'd for Europe & all the artillery & ftores are nearly Embarked & will fail immediately for the Weft Indies—Sir Guy Carleton appears anxious to effect the Evacuation fpeedily—on Saturday laft at dinner he informed me of his determination to move with all poffible expedition and faid that the only thing which detained him was the refugees whofe fituation humanity obliged him to attend to—they are difcharging great numbers of their foldiers many of whom have applyed to me to know whether they can be permitted to remain here—I have taken the Liberty to give them encouragement & muft obferve to your Excellency that in confequence of numberlefs warm publications in our papers and the unconftitutional proceedings of Committees I fuppose not lefs than fifteen thoufand inhabitants will be drove from this Country who are not confcious of any other Crime than that of refiding within the Britifh Lines, fome perhaps have acted tho' in general with reluctance & who I fhould fuppofe might be excufed upon this principle that the fubjects of any State or Country owe allegiance

to the powers under which they reside and are obligated
to lend their affistance when called for in return for protection and the benefits of Society—however this is an
opinion that the people at large will not admit of in confequence of which upon the evacuation we fhall find a City
deftitute of Inhabitants & a fettlement made upon our frontiers by a people whofe minds being fowr'd by the feverity
of their treatment will prove troublefome neighbours and
perhaps lay the foundation of future contefts which I fuppofe would be for the Interelt of our Country to avoid

   I am with great refpect &c

[For Wafhington's Reply, fee "Sparks's Wafhington, Vol. viii., p. 476;
to which Lieut. Col. Smith made anfwer as follows:]

                                    NEW YORK 5th Sepr 1783.
Sir
   I rec'd your Excellency's Letter of the 31ft ulte and
am always particularly happy whenever my conduct meets
with your approbation I muft acknowledge myfelf obliged
by the advice contained in the latter part of the Leter relative to granting Paffports to perfons going into the Country—protections I never prefumed to give—it may not be
improper to inform your Excellency of the principles upon
which I move and the Ideas I hold up to thefe people—
both in public and private converfations I have always held
it as ridiculous for Individuals to be fifhing for the opinion
of their friends refpecting their ftay in this Country—afert-
ing that by applying to their own feelings they may be bet-

10

ter able to determine that I am confident that every perfon found within thofe parts formerly poffeffed by the britifh Troops would be entitled to and receive the protection
of government at leaft from Injury and infult of the people
untill a proper inveftigation can be made refpecting their
Conduct when if it appears that they have in any inftance
run counter to the laws of their Country or extended their
actions further than the perfect right of individuals would
juftify & what they owd to the Goverment under which
they refided they muft expect punifhment adequate to their
Crimes, which I am confident would never be inflicted but
in cafes which Juftice would warrant and which upon examination would tend to confirm and render refpactable
rather than injure our National Character—that the Gentlemen holding the reigns of Civil Goverment have a perfect
Idea of the rights of the Citizen and are attached to the
Conftitution of their Country that at the fame time they
would exert the powers of Goverment to fhelter the mean-
eft Character from perfonal injury the moft exalted need
never flatter himfelf that his wealth or ftation can effect the
opperation of the Laws provided by his Conduct he has
expofed himfelf to their lafh—upon this foundation when
preffed I give my opinion, but have rather been careful in
avoiding political converfations being a fubject which in
general ought to be handled with great delicacy particularly by Military Characters in the prefent fituation of affairs
by the Bearer Enfign Shyter late of the German Troops I

fend the Caps for the Boys Should they prove too large
fmall Cufhions within the Crown will make them fit & fett
eafier than without—the above mentioned Gentleman was
A. C. to Lt Gen¹ De Knoblock has obtained a very honorable difmiffion & intends fettling in this Country.

I am &c

William Stephens Smith, the writer of the above letters filled other pofi-
tions of importance during the ftruggle for American independence, among
which was that of acting commiffary-general of prifoners at Dobbs's Ferry.

At the clofe of the war, when John Adams, afterward Prefident Adams,
was appointed minifter-plenipotentiary to the court of Great Britain, Lieutenant-Colonel Smith was appointed his fecretary of legation.   It was during
his refidence in that capacity at London, that Mr. Smith became the fon-in-
law of Mr. Adams by marriage with his only daughter.

That Mr. Smith enjoyed the efteem of General Wafhington is apparent
from the fact that when, in the year 1798, Wafhington was created by Congrefs lieutenant-general and commander-in-chief of the United States armies,
the name of William S. Smith was immediately propofed by him to the fecretary of war as a brigadier-general, or failing that, as an adjutant-general.
He did not obtain either of thefe appointments, but was made colonel, and
afterward furveyor and infpector of the port of New York.

He was engaged in the expedition under General Miranda, upon the fail-
ure of which he retired to the interior of New York ftate, from whence he
was fent as reprefentative to Congrefs in 1813.   He died in 1816.

CASE OF WILLIAM BUTLER, ESQ., LATE ASSISTANT DEPUTY COMMISSARY GENERAL AT NEW YORK.

[The following appears to have been a cafe which was made up for fub-miffion to the law-officers of the crown, for their decifion refpecting the in-dividual liability, under the treaties, of Mr. Butler, a ftaff-officer under Generals Howe, Clinton, and Carleton, for rent and damages of premifes within the city of New York, which were owned by Whigs who had retired from the city, and occupied by the Britifh officers during their occupation of New York from September, 1776, to November 25, 1783.

It is interefting in itfelf, fimply as a legal paper; but it is efpecially inter-efting from the details of the government of the city while it was under martial law, which it furnifhes to the ftudent of local hiftory; and from the feveral orders, which have been copied at length, and are embraced within it.]

In the beginning of the year 1776, the Rebels (now Americans) ftrongly fortified the City & Ifland of New York & having collected a large body of continental troops & militia, exhibited every appearance of a deter-mined & vigorous defence[1]

But in the month of September following, the kings troops having effected a landing on New York ifland,[2] the

---

[1] The preparations which were made at New York, in the beginning of 1776, for the defence of the city, have been fully defcribed in the "Corre-fpondence of the Provincial Congrefs of New York;" in the "Memoirs of General Lee," pp. 12–15; Booth's "New York," pp. 493–495; and in the extracts of letters in this volume, pp. 82–107.

[2] This landing, which was effected on the fifteenth of September, between Turtle Bay and the city, was attended with fome of the moft difgraceful

rebels made a very precipitate retreat from the city,[1] leaving their cannon & great quantities of military & naval
stores of every kind behind them[2]—most of these stores
were lodged in private warehouses, there being no other
public deposits, than the bridewell[3] & powder house[4]

Nineteen twentieths at least of the inhabitants with their
families & effects had left that city between the latter part
of the year 1775 & the month of June 1776[5] & these persons may be diftinguished under the following heads.

First. Rebels or perfons in oppofition to his Majefty's
government & in civil or military capacities.

Second. Thofe who feared the confequences of remaining in a befieged town.[6]

Third. Thofe who were loyalifts & availed themfelves of
that opportunity to avoid militia duty (which without dif-
tinction all the male inhabitants between fixteen & fixty

scenes of the war—the American troops acting in the moft daftardly manner
before the advance guards of the enemy, and retiring without firing a fhot.

[1] The "precipitation" of the retreat from New York, on the fifteenth
of September, 1776, may be feen from the excellent account of it in Davis's
" Memoirs of Burr," L., pp. 100–106.

[2] "Moft of our heavy cannon, and a part of our ftores and provifions,
which we were about removing, were unavoidably left in the city, though
every means had been ufed to prevent it."—*Gen. Wafhington to Prefident of Congrefs,* 16 *September,* 1776.

[3] The " Old Bridewell" which ftood in the Park.

[4] This powder-houfe ftood on the fouth-weftern bank of " the Frefh-
water," in the vicinity of the interfection of Pearl and Centre ftreets.

[5] See letter of Garifh Harfin to Wm. Radclift, *ante* pp. 85–87.

[6] See letter of Garifh Harfin juft quoted.

years were fubject to) & retired into different parts of the Country—and

Fourth   Some hundreds of perfons who were taken up & fent into confinement, or on parole in different parts of the country by orders of the Generals, Provincial Congrefs, or Committees on account of their loyalty[1]

On taking poffeffion of the city of New York, the Commander in chief was pleafed to direct William Butler Efq to take an account of all the derelict property, & make report every evening of his proceedings to Gen[l] Robertfon then Commander of the City[2]

Mr Butler accordingly took an account of all the property found in the different houfes & ftores, that were abandoned by the proprietors or tenants, & reported in writing to the General (as he had been directed) the quantity & nature of fuch property

A diftribution of the various ftores found in the city was therefore made to the feveral departments and

To the Commiffary General
        Commanding officer of Engineers
        Commiffary of Artillery
        Quarter Mafter General, and   ▪
        Barrack Mafter General

[1] See letter of John Varick, jr., *ante* pp. 91–93.

[2] "General Robertfon, then commander of the city." While he commanded the city he lived in William ftreet, near John, and at 109 Pearl ftreet; while governor of the province, in the Beekman Houfe, near Turtle Bay.

such parts of those stores as came within their respective departments were delivered for his majestys service   The surplus consisting of naval stores were applied to the use of his majestys navy

Accounts were also taken of the vacant dwelling houses & storehouses &c, distinguishing the proprietors whether Rebels or friends to government as far as the persons employed on this duty from their own knowledge or the best information could ascertain

For the purpose of carrying on the business of his majestys naval yard, lots of ground & wharfs were required, as well as dwelling houses and storehouses; the former for the accommodation of the different officers, and their offices, & the latter for the security of public stores & materials.   For this purpose, several houses on the East river, & large lots of ground were inclosed, & in addition to the night guard composed of the artificers employed in the yard, a subaltern's guard from the troops in garrison, was constantly mounted for the protection thereof

On application to the Admiral, the legal proprietors of some of the lots, who were then within the British lines were allowed an annual rent for the same

The different departments of the army, required dwelling houses & store houses, also wharfs & lots of ground contiguous to the rivers for the various purposes of their appointment

Mr Butler was also directed to assist the Quarter Master

General in making & fettling the arrangem^ts of Stores, wharfs &c which being done, to the Commiffary General's department,[1] feveral wharfs & ftorehoufes on the Eaft river, were affigned for the receipt & fecurity of provifions from on board the Tranfports from Europe, & proper houfes for officers.   And on the North or Hudfons River feveral vacant lots of ground contiguous to that river were en-clofed for a forage yard & wharfs on that river were alfo occupied for the landing of fuch forage—

To the other departments were affigned houfes ftores wharfs & lots of ground as near each other as poffible.   It was abfolutely neceffary that the public ftores fhould be near each other on account of the centinels required to pro-tect them, from being fet fire to or plundered

Many of the houfes, ftores & wharfs occupied in the Commiffary Generals department, were the property of per-fons then under the protection of government & faithful fubjects to the King.   On reprefenting their fituation to Danl Chamier Efq^r then Commiffary General, it was agreed that rent for thofe houfes & ftores (the property of fuch loyalifts) fhould be paid, & in order that fuch rent might be fairly & equitably afcertained & fettled, two refpectable & difinterefted Citizens were requefted to value & afcertain the annual rents of fuch ftores: which was ac-cordingly done; & their Certificate declaring the rent of

---

[1] "*The Commiffary-general's department.*"   Daniel Chamier was the commiffary-general of the Britifh forces at that time.

such store &c, & a Certificate from the Deputy Commissary's in whose charge such store &c was, certifying the time the same was occupied in that department, rent was punctually paid, & so continued to be paid until the evacuation of New York in 1783. The residue of the houses, stores & wharfs belonging to Persons without the British Lines, were confidered as Rebel property & occupied as such without any charge to government

After the troops were accommodated with quarters the departments with houses & stores, for the purpofes before mentioned and the different Regiments with stores for their baggage, a great number of houses in different parts of the city remained unappropriated except by the indulgence of the Commander in chief, Commandant or Barrack Master General as Tenants at will, liable to be turned out at a moments warning. A return was therefore ordered to be made of all houses & stores, with the proprietors names, by whom occupied & by whose authority. Alfo the number of fire places & rooms, state & condition of each house, with the street & number.

The Inhabitants from the arrival of his Majesty's Troops till the evacuation of New York in Novr 1783 were freed from the payment of taxes of any kind either for the purpofe of lighting the lamps, or cleaning the city, repairs of the pumps, streets or roads, or other public works, as well as the maintenance of the poor.

The markets were raifed above eight hundred P C^t for

the neceſſaries of life.   The landlords from the demand for houſes raiſed their rents on an average at four times the ſum ſuch houſes had rented previous to the rebellion.   And the vaſt number of merchants & others daily arriving in the city was the cauſe of a conſtant increaſe in the article of houſe rent.

At this time, December 1777, the poor were greatly diſ- treſſed : & General Robertſon then Commandant of New York was pleaſed to appoint nineteen gentlemen from the different wards of the city, to ſolicit contributions for their relief.[1] Thoſe Gentlemen collected ſuch a ſum as afforded a temporary relief.   Theſe gentlemen with the Magiſtrates of Police were then formed into a veſtry & the alms houſe & poor of the city were committed to their care & latterly

[1] The following is a copy of the proclamation under which this committee was appointed, copied from Hugh Gaine's "*New York Gazette: and the Weekly Mercury.*" No. 1366, Monday, Dec. 29, 1777.

By MAJOR GENERAL
JAMES ROBERTSON,
Commandant in the City of New York.

WHEREAS it is repreſented to me that the Poor of this City cannot be properly relieved without ſome Proviſion be made for that Purpoſe, as there is not a veſtry at preſent in this City to aſſeſs the Quotas of the Inhab- itants, and to Superintend the Poor as formerly ; and it appearing to me highly reaſonable that ſome Method ſhould be adopted for their Relief, and *Elias Deſbroſſes, Miles Sherbrooke, Iſaac Low, Charles Nicoll, Gabriel H. Ludlow, James Jauncey, Richard Sharpe, Charles Shaw, Hamilton Young, Theophylact Bache, Rem Rapalje, Jeronimus Alſtyn, William Walton, William Laight, Willett Taylor, William Uſtick, Peter Stuyveſant, Nich- olas Bayard,* and *John Dyckman,* of this City, Gentlemen, having offered

the pumps, lamps &c. This veftry had a Treafurer & Secretary the former to receive & pay monies on their account
& the latter to keep minutes of their proceedings. Proper
funds for the execution of the truft repofed in them were
neceffary—therefore the rents of fuch houfes & ftores as
were not wanted for the fervice of government & the fer-
ries & markets were appropriated to the funds for the veftry—the fees arifing from licenfes & excife, fines inflicted
for breach of orders, Proclamations of the peace, or other
offences were alfo added & ordered to be paid into the
hands of their Treafurer. He was accountable for the payment & receipt of all monies on their account, not only to
the Veftry, but when required, furnifhed the Commander in
Chief & Commandant, with his accounts—When he gave a
receipt for rent fuch receipt fpecified that the fum had been
paid by orders of the Commander in Chief.'

to take upon themfelves the difcharge of the Truft hereinafter repofed in
them : I HAVE therefore thought fit hereby to authorize them to folicit and
receive the Donations of the Charitable and well-difpofed, and to appropriate the fame to the Relief of the Poor, according to their feveral Wants and
Neceffities.

  GIVEN *under my Hand at the City of New York, the 27th Day
of December, in the Eighteenth Year of his Majefty's Reign, Anno Domini,*
1777.

    JAMES ROBERTSON, M. G.
      And Commandant of New York.

 ' It appears from the report of John Smythe, the Collector for the Veftry,
that the " Cafh received for half a Year's Rent, to the 1ft May, laft, (1778)
of Sundry Perfons occupying Houfes to which they had no Claim or Title,
as per Particulars, in the Hands of John Smyth, Efq" was £2244 2s. 10d.,

Whenever the proprietors of houfes fo rented out by the veftry came within the Britifh lines, & made application to the Commandant, their pretenfions were referred to the veftry, & on their report & recommendation, the property was reftored—and

When the Proprietors of houfes or ftores in the king's fervice or barrack department came in, & made fimilar applications their pretenfions were referred to the Magiftrates of Police, & Barrack Mafter & on their report the property was reftored, unlefs in fome inftances, where his Majefty's fervice would not permit.

The wharfs till the firft January 1779 had been occupied by his majefty's Ships & tranfports in government fervice, without paying any wharfage, but as many of them belonged to Loyalifts, it was determined, that on the proprietors making oath as to the property, & that no perfons without the Britifh lines (with an exception in regard to any Copartner in fuch wharf) were interefted or concerned therein the Commandant gave his permiffion to fuch proprietor to occupy his wharf or part of a wharf & receive the ufual & cuftomary wharfage, on condition that fuch proprietor kept the faid wharf in good & fufficient repair.

Capt. Kennedy & Mr. Lefferts owned one of the wharfs in the Commiffary Generals department. Captain Kennedy was allowed & paid by the Commiffary General one dollar

while the expenditures "in removing the Dirt and Filth from the Streets and Barracks, filling up Slips, &c" amounted to £900.

per day for his half: but as Mr. Lefferts was without the Britifh lines, nothing was allowed him. This wharf as well as all others in the Commiffary General's department & the ftores were kept in conftant repair at the expenfe of government. Wages & materials being very high, had the Owners been in full poffeffion of their property & rented the fame for any moderate fum, many of them would have been lofers, had they been obliged to have kept the premifes in repair.

On the 6th day of April 1783 a packet from England arrived at New York & brought over the preliminary articles of peace, & on the 8th of the fame month, his Majeftys proclamn declaring a ceffation of hoftilities, was publicly read by the Town Major at the City hall.

. Before the arrival of the preliminary articles viz: on the 18th February His Excellency Sir Guy Carleton' iffued a general order in thefe words—

"Orders Head Quarters, New York Feb 18 1783 Should "there be any perfon, at prefent within the lines, whofe "houfes or lands have been withheld from them on account "of offences or fuppofed offences againft the Crown, they

<hr/>

[1] Sir Guy Carleton was a major-general in 1772; in 1774 he was appointed Captain-General and Governor of Canada, where he commanded during the campaign of 1775-6, under Generals Montgomery and Arnold. In 1782 he fucceeded Sir Henry Clinton, as commander-in-chief of his majefty's forces in America; and at the clofe of the war he returned to England, where he fucceeded to the titles and eftate of Lord Dorchefter. He died in 1808, aged eighty-three years.

"are defired to make their refpective claims to the Officers
"of Police in New York on Longland or on Staten
"ifland, who will report the fame to the Commander in
"chief. All perfons without the lines, who have aban-
"doned Eftates within are defired to fend their claims to the
"offices of police aforefaid, and all perfons occupying Ef-
"tates within the above defcriptions, are ftrictly enjoined to
"take due care thereof, as they will be made anfwerable for
"any damage, wafte or deftruction, that may henceforward
"be committed on the fame. They will likewife permit
"any perfon authorized from either of the above mentioned
"offices to vifit the faid Eftates, & take Inventories of all
"effects thereunto belonging.

"O. L. DELANCEY Adjutant General.'"

Another order was afterward iffued in thefe words

"New York 27 March 1783— Orders—In order to fave
"much unneceffary trouble Notice is hereby given. That no
"perfons whatever are to be admitted into the Britifh Lines,
"without having previoufly obtained Paffports for that pur-
"pofe from the Commandant except thofe who come to &
"go from the markets. They will report themfelves to
"the Police, whofe permiffions to take out horfes &c will

[1] Oliver L. De Lancey, fon of General Oliver De Lancey, of New York. He succeeded Major André, as adjutant-general of the army. He became, fubfequently, deputy-adjutant-general of England, barrack-mafter-general of the Britifh army, a member of Parliament, and a lieutenant-general of the army; and died in Edinburgh in 1820.

" be fufficient—Any perfons who may have come in with-
" out leave are directed to report themfelves immediately at
" the Commandants office, otherwife they will be fubject to
" very difagreeable confequences. The General officers
" commanding in the feveral diftricts, will fee that particular
" attention is paid to this order by the officers at the out-
" pofts.

" O. L. DeLancey Adjutant General."

Thefe orders were iffued prior to the arrival of the preliminary articles. many perfons (who had been very active
during the rebellion) were in confequence admitted within
the Britifh lines & in conforming to the mode prefcribed in
thefe orders were permitted to view their Eftates, take Inventories & unmolefted or infulted to return.

After the arrival of the preliminary articles fome hundreds (if not thoufands) of perfons who had been in oppofition to his majefty's government were allowed free ingrefs
& regrefs to & from New York on obtaining paffports for
that purpofe, which were eafily obtained on the application
of their friends   But many perfons whofe only crime was
that of loyalty to their Sovereign, on going a few miles
into the Country without the Britifh Lines, were feverely
punifhed & obliged to return, not being permitted to vifit
their relations & friends after an abfence of fome years.

A number of refugees under the command of Major
Ward who glorioufly defended the Blockhoufe' at Bull's

---

¹ The attack on the block-houfe at Bull's Ferry, July 20, 1780, was one of

Ferry on the 20 July 1780 againſt a very ſuperior force of the enemy in the autumn of the year 1782 propoſed to the Commander in chief to remove & ſettle in the Province of Nova Scotia, on lands to be granted them & proviſions & ſome other aid from government. He acceded to their propoſal, & about ſix hundred men, women & children embarked for that province in the latter part of that year.

After the arrival of the preliminary articles & before the definitive Treaty arrived, from the vindictive & perſecuting diſpoſition of the Americans, the refugees & other Loyaliſts were cut off from all hope of remaining in the States after the Britiſh troops ſhould be withdrawn. They therefore made application to Sir Guy Carlton to be tranſported with their families & effects to Nova Scotia, on the ſame terms as the other refugees had gone there, that under the protection of his Majeſty's government, they might find an aſylum from the tyranny & oppreſſion of their Countrymen. They were accordingly ſent to ſuch parts of that province as they requeſted. In conſequence of ſuch removal many of the derelict Eſtates became vacant, whereupon the Commander in chief was pleaſed to iſſue the following order

Head Quarters New York 16 June 1783   Orders

" The proprietors of houſes or lands lately evacuated will " apply to Lieut Genˡ Campbell for the poſſeſſion of thoſe

the moſt deſperate affairs of the war. It has not received that place in our hiſtorical annals which its importance demands.

" on Long ifland, To Brigadier General Birch for thofe on
" York ifland & to Brigadier General Bruce[1] for thofe on
" Staten ifland.   Thefe General officers will be pleafed to
" caufe all fuch Eftates to be immediately delivered up to
" the Proprietors or their attorneys unlefs where they may
" fee fufficient reafons for detaining them fome time longer,
" which reafons they will report to the Commander in chief.
" In like manner, all Eftates which fhall hereafter be evac-
" uated are to be furrendered up to the proprietors.
" O. L. De Lancey Adjutant General "

From the 16th of June to the day of evacuation of New
York the property which had been from time to time
vacated was reftored to the proprietors.   But many houfes
& ftores abfolutely neceffary were detained from the Proprietors until the evacuation of the city.   Every pains was
taken to prevent wafte or deftruction or improper perfons
from poffeffing fuch houfes after the then poffeffors fhould
have left them as will appear from the following garrifon
order iffued by Brigadier General Birch Commandant of
New York

" Garrifon orders 29 April 1783   In order to prevent
" any wafte or deftruction in the houfes under the direction
" of the veftry or Barrack office notice is hereby given
" that the prefent poffeffors of houfes under the above
" defcription are on no account to quit them, without giv-

---

[1] *Brigadier-general Bruce*, probably Andrew Bruce of the 54th Foot.

21

" ing previous notice to the Commandant, that an ex-
" amination may be made into their ftate; & on removal
" the keys are to be lodged at his office No 61 Wall
" Street; any perfon prefuming to take poffeffion of fuch
" houfes, without permiffion from the Commandant, muft
" expect the moft difagreeable confequences. By order of
" the Commandant

" E. WILLIAMS Major of Brigade"[1]

In order that juftice might be done & that all perfons
who had any claims on the Britifh government, during the
time his Majeftys troops were in that part of North America now called the United States, & that the equity of the
claims of fuch public creditors might be fully inveftigated
his excellency Sir Guy Carlton was pleafed to iffue the
following orders.

Head Quarters N York 4 May 1783. Orders—

" As many claims & demands have been exhibited to the
" Commander in chief for property fupplied to the Britifh
" army or officers in the feveral public departments fince
" the 19th day of April 1775 & as it is expedient that the
" nature, extent & validity of fuch claims & demands
" fhould be known & afcertained in order that right &
" juftice may be adminiftered—Gregory Townfhend Efq[r]

---

[1] E. Williams, brigade-major; probably Elijah Williams, of Deerfield,
Maffachufetts, who had entered the army in 1775; retired on half-pay after
peace was reftored; and died in 1793.

" Affiftant Commiffary General,' Captain Armftrong Deputy
" Quarter General, Ward Chipman Efq^r,² Richard Harrifon
" Efq^r & Mr John Hamilton Agent³ are appointed a Board
" of Commiffioners, to receive & examine all fuch claims &
" demands, to call for & inveftigate the proofs that may be
" exhibited thereof, & to regifter the fame preparatory to a
" farther liquidation.   The faid Commiffioners or any three
" of them are authorized & directed to meet for the above
" purpofe, at fuch place & on fuch days & times as they
" may deem proper   All fuch perfons having fuch claims
" & demands, are to exhibit the fame with the proofs &
" vouchers before this Board"

O. L. DELANCY Adjutant General

This Board met from the time of their appointment &
continued to meet, till within a very fhort time before the
evacuation of New York & many claims & demands
againft the army & public departments prefented to them.
Many of thofe claimants were defired to call for their
papers by advertifements in thefe words

" Board of claims 28 October 1783.   The undermen-

¹ Gregory Townfhend, Efq., affiftant-commiffary-general, probably a refugee from Bofton, who had been driven from that town in 1778.

² Ward Chipman, Efq., a refugee from Bofton who had entered the army
as deputy-mufter-mafter-general of the loyalift forces.   After the war clofed
he retired to New Brunfwick, where he became a member of the Affembly,
advocate-general, folicitor-general, chief juftice of the Supreme Court, and
prefident and acting governor.   He died at Fredericton in 1824.

³ John Hamilton ; fee Note 2, page 127.

" tioned Perfons who left papers with this board are defired
" to call at No 32 Queen Street.   By order.

" ROBᵗ N. AUCHMUTY Secry"

All the before mentioned orders were printed in the public Newfpapers & continued to be publifhed for many
months fucceffively—

The following advertifement, which is but a repetition of
that which had been frequently publifhed even before the
peace will fhew the intention of the Commiffary General to
do juftice to all perfons having any demands on his department

Commiffary General's office, New York 13th Novʳ 1783

" All perfons having demands againft the Commiffary
" Generals department, for provifions, fuel, forage, ftore-rent,
" veffel hire &c are defired to call & receive payment for
" the fame before the 22ᵈ Inft. after which no moneys will
" be paid."

In the fixth article of the Definitive Treaty, it is declared
" That there fhall be no future confifcations made, nor any
" profecutions commenced againft any perfon or perfons for
" or by reafon of the part which he or they may have taken
" in the prefent war: & that no perfon fhall on that account
" fuffer any lofs or damage either in his perfon, liberty or
" property, & that thofe who may be in confinement on
" fuch charges, at the time of the ratification of the treaty
" in America fhall be immediately fet at liberty, & the pro-
" fecution fo commenced be difcontinued"

And although the Definitive Treaty is but an echo of the preliminary articles, which arrived in America in the month of April 1783 yet the Legiflature of the State of New York had on the 17th day of March in that year, paffed an act of which the following is a copy & which act is unrepealed.

"An Act for granting a more effectual relief in cafes of "certain trefpaffes. Be it enacted by the people of the "State of New York reprefented in Senate & Affembly, & "it is hereby enacted by the authority of the fame That it "fhall & may be lawful for any perfon or perfons who are "or were inhabitants of this ftate & who by reafon of the "invafion of the enemy left his, her or their place or places "of abode, & who have not voluntarily put themfelves "refpectively into the power of the enemy, fince they re- "fpectively left their places of abode, his, her or their Heirs "Executors or Adminiftrators, to bring an action of Trefpafs "againft any perfon or perfons, who may have occupied, in- "jured or deftroyed his, her or their Eftate, either real or "perfonal, within the power of the enemy, or againft any "perfon or perfons who fhall have purchafed or received "any fuch goods or effects, or againft his, her or their Heirs, "Ex'ors or Adm'ors in any court of record within this "State having cognizance of the fame, in which action, if "the fame fhall be brought againft the perfon or perfons, "who have occupied, injured, or deftroyed, or purchafed or "received fuch real or perfonal Eftate as aforefaid, the "Defendant or Defendants fhall be held to bail, & if any

" fuch action fhall be brought in any inferior Court, within
" this ftate, the fame fhall be finally determined in fuch
" Court, & every fuch action fhall be confidered as a tranfi-
" tory action.   That no Defendant or Defendants fhall be
" admitted to plead in juftification any military order or
" command whatever of the enemy for fuch occupancy, in-
" jury, deftruction, purchafe or receipt, nor give the fame in
" evidence on the general iffue"[1]

Mr Butler having fettled all his public & private accounts in the month of June 1781. obtained the Commander in chief & Commiffary General's leave to come to
England, & has not fince that time been in America   And
at that time, both countries were at war, & the garrifon of
New York was in the poffeffion of his Majefty's Troops:
& all perfons civil & military & all property & in all parts
of the Britifh lines, were fubject to, & under the abfolute
controul of the Commander in chief—

    " On the 24th day of May laft, the Legiflature of the
" State of New York paffed an Act entitled an Act to amend
" an Act entitled an Act for relief againft abfconding or ab-
" fent Debtors; & to extend the remedy of the act entitled
" an act for granting a more effectual relief in cafes of cer-
" tain trefpaffes & for other purpofes therein mentioned"[2]

[1] Chap. xxxi., Laws of 1783.   This is the fo-called Trefpafs Act of New
York.

[2] Mr. Butler was in error concerning the date of this law.   It was paffed
on the *fourth* of May, 1784, and is known as Chap. liv. of the Laws
of New York, Seventh Seffion.—1 *Greenleaf*, 114.

A copy of this act cannot at prefent be procured but the mode of proceeding on that act is fully pointed out in the advertifements in the New York papers & which in fub-ftance is as follows   A. B. gives notice That in purfuance of that act, an action of Trefpafs had been by him commenced againft C. D. in the Mayors court of the City of New York, that the Writ in the faid caufe had been returned, not found, by the Sheriff, that a declaration was thereupon filed in the Clerks office of the City of New York againft the faid C. D. by the faid A. B. agreeable to the mode preferibed in & by the faid act "for the ufe & " occupation of a dwelling houfe, with the appurtenances of " the faid A. B. by him the faid C. D. during the late war " between the United States of America & Great Britain, & " while the City of New York was in the poffeffion of the " fleets & armies of the King of Great Britain" and that it was thereby publifhed & notified that unlefs the faid C. D. entered his appearance in the *faid action* within fix months from the date of that advertifement, a judgment would be entered againft the faid C. D. & a writ of inquiry would be granted to afcertain the faid A. B's demand againft the C. D. for the trefpaffes aforefaid agreeable to the intention & meaning of the faid act & the practice of the faid Court.

Mr Butler happens to be one of the few Officers employed in his Majeftys fervice, who has left any eftate in the province of New York & four fuits have been commenced

againit him, under the lait mentioned act, of which actions,
notice has been given in the terms above mentioned

The firlt of thefe fuits is brought by Mr Lefferts already
mentioned : the caufe of action for the ufe & occupation of
a dwelling houfe & dock with the appurtenances of the
faid Jacob Lefferts. The fecond is by a William Smith,
for the ufe & occupation of a dwelling houfe with the appurtenances of the faid William Smith.   The third is by a
Thomas Henderfon, as well for the ufe & occupation of one
dwelling houfe, ftore houfe & dock with the appurtenances
as for the deftruction of one ftore houfe, & diverfe quantities
of houfehold & kitchen furniture of the faid Thomas Henderfon by the faid Will: Butler   And the fourth is by a
Tho⁵ Ivers' for taking & carrying away of diverfe new
cables, a large quantity of cordage, nails, hemp, black tar,
pitch, & feveral utenfils & tools commonly ufed in the
rope making bufinefs, the property of the faid Thomas
Ivers by him the faid Will: Butler. It is of little confequence to enter into an inquiry with refpect to the fituation
of the feveral Plaintiffs in thefe fuits   Mr Butler had left
the feat of war a length of time before there was the leaft
profpect of peace & had he remained until the final evacuation, his perfon & property were equally free & and indem-
nified by the preliminary articles & the Definitive treaty, if
thofe Treaties had any validity, or there can be any public
faith or honour in the ftates.   But it has been lately deter-

---

¹ Thomas Ivers was one of the popular " Committee of One Hundred."

mined in the Mayors Court of New York, that all who held houses under the authority of the Commander in chief should be exempted from the repayment of rent: but that those who held under the Commissary general should be liable, because he had no authority by the laws of war to raise a revenue, but that his power was usurped.

As Mr. Butler during the whole of the time he served in America, acted only in a subordinate capacity & under the orders of his superiors namely the Commander in Chief & Commandant, to whose orders, he & all others in the different departments were bound to pay implicit obedience besides the orders of the head of that department

It is therefore asked

1mo Shall Mr. Butler in his private capacity be answerable for things done in his official character & in conformity to the orders of his superiors?

2do Supposing the Crown indebted to the Plaintiffs in those suits, for the articles charged, shall his private fortune be answerable for these demands?

3^{tio} Do not the proceedings in those causes defeat the Definitive Treaty[1] & are not the Acts on which those suits are brought violations of the faith of the United States pledged on signing the preliminary articles & executing the Definitive Treaty?

4to What steps he ought to pursue & whether it would

---

[1] The Definitive Treaty of Peace may be found, at length, in the "Journal of the Congress of the United States," January 14, 1784.

22

not be advisable to enter his appearance to defend those suits?

5ᵗᵒ Whether if he omits making any defence & suffers judgment to go against him, he can claim compensations for any loss or damage he may sustain, by reason of such judgment?

Account of Houses, Lands, Debts & effects the property of William Butler in the City & province of New York which he was obliged to leave.

Bayard's Purchase on the Mohawk River.

In this tract Mr B. had 1050 Acres, for which he was offered 8s. P acre

Curry.

420   0   0

Delaware Tract

This Tract lies between the River Delaware & the Susquehannah, adjoining to lands belonging to General Provost & the Honᵇˡᵉ Henry White Lawrence Cartwright Esqʳ & others for which has been offered in peaceable times 6s P acre for the whole—Mr Butler's share of this tract is one entire piece containing 3994 acres, say a 6s

1198   4   0

Butter Hill Tract

This Tract lies on the West side of Hudsons river & within half a mile of it & about

Carried forward   1618   4   0

Brought forward   1618   4   0

fixty miles from New York. This land is well known by the name of the Clove, as it lies between the two great hills known by the names of Great Butter Hill & Little Butter Hill. It contains 632 acres for which Mr B was offered 16s P acre   505 12   0

Forest of Dean Tract [1]

Lies within 3 miles of the above Tract, & contains 362 acres of land with the very best timber. It is known by the name of the Black Swamp & is within 3 miles of the river, between the iron works of Col[l] Matthews & Mr Hauienclever[2] & was always valued a 20s P acre   362   0   0

The Mine Tract

Lies within 7 miles of New Windfor & Newburgh & contains 120 acres of land bought of Mr Golett[3] a merchant in New

Carried forward   2485 16   0

[1] Foreft of Dean in the lower part of the Highlands, north from Haverftraw, between that village and Fort Montgomery.

[2] Mr. Heffenclever's iron works were in the upper part of what is now Rockland county. This gentlemen had expended large amounts of money in attempting to eftablifh iron-works; and he had received the favorable confideration of the colonial authorities for his enterprife and perfeverance.

[3] Probably Mr. Peter Goelet, a member of "the Committee of One Hundred," and grandfather of Peter Goelet, Efq., who refides at the corner of Broadway and Eaſt Nineteenth ſtreet, in this city.

Brought forward   2485 16   0

York in the year 1772 for which Mr B paid
them 17s P acre   102   0   0

Poughkepſey

This Tract lies in the middle of the Town,
within a quarter of a mile of the Courthouſe
& joins the Glebe land. It contains 210 acres
for which W. B. was offered 40s P acre   This
land is within 60 miles of New York   420   0   0

Ten Stone Meadow

This tract lies 7 miles weſt of Hudſon's
River & is known by the name of Newburgh Ridge, about 7 miles diſtant from
Newburgh & New Windſor   It adjoins to
the lands of John Leake Eſq[r] & others &
contains 270 acres for which 40s P acre has
been offered   540   0   0

Sachandaga Tract

This Tract lies on the Sachandaga river
in the County of Albany about 15 miles
from Sir John Johnſton's[2]   It contains in all
52000 acres of which W. B. was to have
12000   This Land was bought from the

Carried forward   3547 16   0

[1] John Leake, one of the founders of the Leake and Watts Orphan Houſe
at Bloomingdale.

[2] Sir John Johnſon's—"Johnſon Hall," near the village of Johnſtown,
Fulton county, New York.

Brought forward   3547 16 0

Indians about the year 1770 or 1771 in the names of Col^l Butler, Hendrick Benfon, Durck Lefferts, John & Robt Leake Co. for which the Indians were paid £12 P thoufand   By fome means or other, the patent from government did not iffue: & the troubles beginning there was no way of obtaining it, as the Governor was obliged to come away—W. B. paid for 12000 acres of the above Tract at £12 P thoufand which makes the amo^t of his claim to be   144 0 0

Lechacticook Lands

Thefe Lands lie on the Eaft fide of Hudfon's River, oppofite to the Half moon, 12 miles north of the City of Albany, & contain 840 acres, which were proved vacant & granted by the Governor & Council of New York on or about the year 1769 to Robt Leake Co. Thefe Lands were held in poffeffion by Anth'y Bratt Hendrick Vrouman & others, who rather than move off bought them at 20s per acre & paid £100 down to bind the bargain. The remaining £740 was to be paid in three annual payments with in-

Carried forward   3691 61 0

Brought forward   3691 16   0

tereſt   W. B⁵ claim is for one fourth of £840 the ſum that it ſold for to the above purchaſers

210   0   0

Two Lots of Land at the River ſide near the College at New York[1]

The eligible ſituation of the place, induced Mr B. & others to make this ground which they verily did entirely—& the firſt ſtep towards it, was by obtaining a grant from the Governors of the College into the river from high water mark to low water mark, an extent of 100 feet   They then dug into the ſide of the hill 75 feet by 60 & with horſes & carts carried the earth to the front which was incloſed by the wharf; ſo that when the lots were completely finiſhed they meaſured 60 feet in front on the river & 157 deep on the land ſide.   The wharf in front coſt Mr B. £60.   The front fence & a ſmall houſe in the garden coſt him £60 & he was offered £100 with the above expence for each of the lots.   When the Kings troops arrived at Staten iſland, the Roſe & Phenix²' men of

Carried forward   3901 16   0

[1] King's (*now Columbia*) College, New York.
[2] The Roſe and Phenix, with three tenders, paſſed up the river, as ſtated

Brought forward	3901	16	0

war were ordered up the North river: &
the Rebels in order to annoy them thought
proper to erect a battery on my ground,[1] for
which purpose they filled up my wharf & all
the post & timber on the lots—by which their
purpose was anfwered but afterwards by taking up the wharf, the water in a fhort time
flowed in & wafhed all away, by which means,

he loft what he might have obtained that is	320	0	0
Debts due as p abftract	800	0	0

Houfes

A fine lot of Lot ground in New York
fituated on the Eaft river, on which there is a
new Brick houfe in front & a wooden houfe
in the rear called Montgomy Ward, for
which Eftate Mr. B. paid down in ready
Cafh in the year 1781 to Hugh Gain Printer

at New York[2] 750 guineas—equal to	1340	0	0
Carried forward	6361	16	0

in the text; and very minute accounts of their trip may be found in General Wafhington's "Letter to General Schuyler," July 15, 1776, and in
Irving's "Life of Wafhington," II., pp. 259–264.

[1] "In the year 1776, when the Phœnix and Rofe frigates pufhed up the
North River, the Americans made a tremendous fire from this battery (*Fort
George*) *and the others along the North river*, from as many as two hun-
dred cannons."—Old Magazine, cited by Mr. Watfon (Annals, p. 334).

[2] Hugh Gaine, printer; the veteran publifher of "The New York Ga-

Brought forward   6361 16 0

A fine lot of ground, on which there are two good houses situate at the Corner of Maiden Lane & William Street in the East ward of the City of New York. for which Mr B paid in 1781 to Robt Deal, merchant, in ready money 700 guineas—equal to   1306 13 4

Negroes left behind by Mr. B

A man   —   cost £65
A woman   —   do   45
A boy 2 years old   10   120 0 0

N. B. Mr B. could not bring away many valuable effects which are here omitted—

£7788 9 4

[Endorsed
        Case of Wm Butler Esq.]

zette and Mercury." As may be seen by reference to page 34, his place of business was in Hanover square.

WASHINGTON'S CONTEMPLATED ATTACK ON NEW YORK.

[The following paper, part of which, in the original, is in the autograph of Sir Henry Clinton, appears to be a statement of some of the circumstances which induced that gentleman to permit the allied forces of America and France to proceed from the North to Virginia, without interruption; and it is a partial defence of his conduct against the censures which were thrown upon it after the capture of Lord Cornwallis at Yorktown.

The person to whom it was addressed, it appears, desired to use the information for some public purpose; and it is not improbable that, whoever he was, he had seen service in America, under Sir Henry's command.

The subject of the paper has been fully and ably discussed in the spicy correspondence between Sir Henry Clinton and Lord Cornwallis, which was published in London in 1783.]

If a Question should be asked respecting a possibility of attacking Washington in July and August,[1] in few Words I say—

1st. He had at least, with the French,[2] 11.000—I had of

---

[1] At the time to which this paper refers—July and August, 1781—General Washington was meditating a formidable descent upon New York for the purpose of taking it from Sir Henry Clinton, who was believed (a belief this paper tends to confirm) to have so weakened himself by detachments to the southward, as to render the success of such an important enterprise practicable, supported as Washington expected to be by the French fleet under Count de Graffe. A letter, however, reached Washington from De Graffe, on the 14th of August, stating that the latter would sail directly for the Chesapeake—which decided Washington to co-operate with him there against Lord Cornwallis.

[2] Count de Rochambeau was supporting Washington with the French forces from Newport.

23

Regular Troops, altogether 9.300 fit for Duty,[1] & thefe difperfed in an Extent of above 100 miles—To affemble them would require Days—to do it wantonly, expofe all the different Stations, delay the Works then carrying on &c &c &c

As to the objeĉt, Wafhington 12 miles from me[2] with 11,000 men in a Pofition exceeding ſtrong, and if beat finding another within a Mile & &c[3] fuch an attack not juſtifiable with five times the force I could, after taking care of thefe important Stations, ſpare.   For of 9.300 it was in formal Council of Generals Kniphaufen[4] Robertfon[6]

---

[1] " Had my correfpondence been produced, it would have appeared from it, and the returns accompanying it, that inſtead of feventeen, twenty, nay, twenty-four thoufand men, which it has been reported I had at New York (after the very ample reinforcements, as the Miniſter acknowledges, which I had fent to the fouthward), I had not 12,000 effeĉtives, and of thefe not above 9500 fit for duty, regulars and Provincials."—*Sir Henry Clinton's Narrative*, 1783, p. 12.

[2] The head quarters of General Wafhington were " near Dobbs's Ferry," although the encampments of the allied armies extended to the eaſtward as far as the White Plains.

[3] It is probable " the Hills" in North Caſtle—to which General Wafhington had fallen back in the fall of 1776, after the battle of the White Plains —is the pofition here referred to.

[4] General Knyphaufen commanded the Heſſian troops in America.   He retired to Pruſſia at the clofe of the war, and died at Berlin, in June, 1789, aged 59 years.

[5] General James Robertfon was appointed major of the firſt battalion of the fixtieth regiment, in December, 1755; and in May, 1758, deputy quarter-maſter-general in America.   He was prefent at the fiege of Louiſbourg, in 1758; was appointed lieutenant-colonel, July 8, 1758; accompanied General Amherſt up to the northern frontiers, in 1759, as quartermaſter-general;

and Birch agreed that I could not pafs beyond the Harlem, with any probability of remaining a few days, without I left of Regular Troops 6.500. All agreeing that thefe Pofts could not be trufted to Militia.' By which it appears that I had for forward movement not quite 3.000 of Regular Troops. But I am free to own that if I had had four times that number I would not have marched out to attack Wafhington's Army fo pofted, and in a great meafure Mafter of the Rivers with his Gun Boats &c For we had not a fingle Frigate in them, ignorant where our Fleet were gone, or when it might return, and by no means certain that the French Fleet might not vifit us: befides all this, I expected daily reinforcement from England² and Cheafa-

was appointed lieutenant-colonel of the 55th regiment, October, 29, 1759; was with the expedition againft Martinico, in 1762; and in 1772 was promoted to colonel in the army. On the 1ft January, 1776, being at Bofton, he was appointed a major-general in America; and on the 11th of the fame month, colonel commanding the 60th regiment. When the enemy evacuated Bofton, he gained an unenviable notoriety from his peculations. He accompanied General Howe to New York; was prefent at the battle of Long Ifland; was appointed commandant in the city of New York; and returned to England in February, 1777. He was appointed a major-general, Auguft 29, 1777; colonel of the 16th regiment, on the 14th May, 1778; on the 4th May, 1779, governor of the colony of New York. He became lieutenant-general, 20th November, 1782; embarked at New York for England, April 15, 1783; and died in 1788.

¹ "I do not know that, after leaving fufficient garrifons in the iflands and pofts depending (*which it is admitted by all would take* 6000) I cou.d, as has been infinuated, have prevented the junction between Mons. Rochambeau and General Wafhington."—*Sir Henry Clinton's Narrative,*" 1783, p. 13.

² Admiral Digby, with fix fhips of the line, arrived at New York on the

peak;[1] by the arrival of which, if in any time, and the
Naval Force that would accompany them, I might attempt
a Move againſt Waſhington with advantage, by deſtroying
his Bridges on Crotees,[2] and place myſelf on his communi-
cations with North Caſtle[3]—You know my place—nor was
this the only objecſt. You know what my views were
about the French Fleet at Rhode Iſland, and, if reinforced
either from Cheaſapeak or England, what I ſhould attempt whenever the Admiral would maſk the Harbour;
for I aſked nothing more of the Fleet.

As to the reconnoitring party of the 5th July you know
how it ended.[4] In the ſituation I was, I could not have
followed it without riſking a general Action with the Garri-
ſon of Kingſbridge only, for I had not time to bring up
more.

twenty-fourth of September, 1781.—*Vide* Sir Henry Clinton's Narrative,
1783, p. 11 ; and Sir Henry Clinton's Letter to General Cornwallis, September 6, 1781.

[1] " Thinking that he (*Lord Cornwallis*) might well ſpare three thouſand
I deſired he would keep all that were neceſſary for a reſpectable defenſive,
and deſultory water movements, and *ſend me of three thouſand men all he
could.*"—*Sir Henry Clinton's Narrative,* 1783, p. 21. See alſo Sir Henry's
Letter to Lord Cornwallis, June 15, 1781.

[2] " Croton River."

[3] North Caſtle, a town in Weſtcheſter county, north-eaſt from the White
Plains, into which the American army retreated after the battle of White
Plains, in October, 1776.—Bolton's " Hiſtory of Weſt Cheſter County," I.
p. 468.

[4] An account of this intereſting affair can be found in General Waſhington's letter to the Preſident of Congreſs, 6 July, 1781 ; and in General
Waſhington's Diary, July 2d and 3d, 1781.

As to the 25th July. By an unexpected Move they mafked our only Debouchee: and while they held it, 30,000 ought not to have tried to force it: but fuppofing I had determined to pafs the Harlem, could I do it before Bridges were thrown over? for to land in Boats would fubject myfelf to be beat in detail; but could I have poffeffed the Heights of Fordam' in force, I recollect my Debouchee. to attack Wafhington in his pofition of Valentine's Houfe[2] (which you have feen) do you think that I could be juftified in attacking him with double his number in fuch a pofition, where fuccefs could not be decifive, and where defeat would be too much fo? nor after that Council of War, could it be fuppofed I would ever leave thefe Stations with much lefs than 6.000.[3] The only chance I ever had of an Attempt upon any part of Wafhington's Army muft have been a partial action, with one or two of his columns advancing to Kingfbridge when I fhould be reinforced.

The German recruits arrived on the 11th Auguft:[4] on the

[1] "*The Heights of Fordham,*" in the town of Weft Farms, Weftchefter county, N. Y.

[2] "*Valentine's Houfe,*" the refidence of Thomas Valentine, on the well-known "Valentine's Hill," about 2½ miles from the village of Yonkers, Weftchefter county, N. Y.—Bolton's "Hiftory of Weftchefter county," II., p. 436.

[3] *Vide* Note 1, page 179.

[4] "A fleet of twenty fail came in laft Saturday with troops, but they are faid to be Heffian recruits from Europe."—*General Wafhington to General La Fayette,* 15 *Auguft,* 1781.

17ᵗʰ Wafhington foraged within fix Miles of me—I expected him again about the 19ᵗʰ or 20ᵗʰ and you know I was prepared to try any experiment that might offer. The Troops were affembled, the materials for Bridges on the ground, and all would have been ready to move over Harlem the 19ᵗʰ. I confulted with Gen¹ Kniphaufen what we fhould do—He feemed I confefs to think that " Le jeu ne valoit pas la chandelle." But I was defirous with 7000 men to try an experiment, as I was perfuaded I could do it with fome fecurity with three Bridges over the Harlem, if it was attempted before Wafhington came too near me all was prepared but the Enemy retired the 19ᵗʰ &c &c &c¹

I mention thefe circumftances not becaufe I can fuppofe any Military man of common fenfe or knowledge of my force, and that of the Enemy or the ground between us, would have fuppofed it poffible for me to have attempted anything, but becaufe I know there is a fet of difcontented animals here, fome of them Military that are determined to critifize *all I do*—You may not probably think it neceffary to fay a fyllable on the fubject, but fhould that be fo, thefe are my Opinions. I could name 1000 more   the above are fome of the Chief.

As to following W—— when he went to the South-

¹ "About noon, His Excellency General Wafhington left the army, fetting his face towards his native State, in full confidence, to ufe his own words, 'with a common bleffing,' of capturing Lord Cornwallis and his army."— *Heath's Memoirs, Auguft 19, 1781.*

ward,' my Letter of the 2ᵈ September to Lord Cornwallis²
proves, how abfurd that would have been; by that I bound
myfelf to reinforce his Lordfhip by every means in my power,
as foon as the Admiral fhould fignify to me it could be done.
To have landed in the Jerfeys would have taken ten days,
by attempting an unimportant Move, I might have loft, the
opportunity of making, the moft important one that could
be made.

N. B. When Mʳ Graves failed,³ Sir Samuel Hood⁴ was
clear of opinion *La Graffe*⁵ would bring no more than 16 of
the Line at moft.⁶ Barras tho' at Sea was far to the Eaſt-

¹ General Wafhington, in his movement againft Cornwallis in Virginia.

² This letter can be found in "The Correfpondence between Sir Henry
Clinton and Earl Cornwallis, relative to the Defence of York, in Virginia."

³ "*Mr. Graves*"—Admiral Lord Graves entered the navy when very
young; was fent to the American ftation in 1761; in 1779, was promoted
to the poft of rear-admiral; in 1793, to that of vice-admiral; and in 1794,
to that of admiral. He was prefent in the action off St. Vincent, and
died March 8, 1787, in the feventy-fourth year of his age.

⁴ "*Sir Samuel Hood*"—Admiral Lord Vifcount Hood, "the Subduer of
Corfica, who firft fhook the enfanguined power of The Mad Deftroyer," was
one of the moft diftinguifhed officers of the Britifh navy. He was employed
in the Weft Indies, where he preferved St. Chriftopher's from being taken by
De Graffe, and was prefent at the famous defeat of that officer by Admiral
Rodney, April 12, 1782. He died at Bath in 1816.

⁵ "*La Graffe*"—Count De Graffe was born in France in 1723; was
appointed to co-operate with the Americans in 1781; and died in 1738.
His daughter married Mr. Depeau, of New York, and his defcendants are
among the moft refpected merchants in that city.

⁶ As will be feen from General Wafhington's letter to the Prefident of
Congrefs, 5th September, 1781, the admiral brought in "*twenty-eight fhips
of the line.*"

ward, there therefore was every probability that Mr Graves would beat them en detail, and even should they join, Sir Samuel Hood faid he thought they were a Match.

Arnold went to new London, the firft of September and returned the 9th[1] in his abfence it was not thought poffible to move a man either by Sea or Land. (It is fuppofed he had all the Tranfports with him. But this is only con-jecture.)

[1] It was not until the 2d of September that Sir Henry Clinton[2] fufpected Wafhington's real deftination, when he defpatched General Benedict Arnold againft New London on the 4th of September. A minute account of that fanguinary vifit of the traitor-general to his native ftate, may be found in "The Battles of the United States," by Henry B. Dawfon, I., pp. 721–723.

[2] Sir Henry Clinton, K. B., was the eldeft fon of Admiral George Clinton, formerly governor of the colony of New York. He entered the army at an early age, as captain-lieutenant in the New York companies. On the 1ft November, 1751, he became lieutenant in the Coldftream Guards; on the 6th May, 1758, captain in the 1ft Foot Guards; in 1762, a colonel in the army; and on the 28th November, 1766, colonel of the 16th regiment. He ferved, with great credit, in the feven years' war in Germany; on the 25th May, 1772, was made a major-general; and in May, 1775, arrived at Bofton. He was prefent when the action on Bunker's Hill was fought, and greatly diftinguifhed himfelf—receiving knighthood and the office of lieuten-ant-general in America. On the 1ft January, 1776, he was made general in America; fuffered defeat on Sullivan's Ifland, in June of that year; was in the battles of Long Ifland and White Plains, and at the capture of Fort Wafhington. In 1777 he commanded on the Hudfon, and captured Forts Montgomery and Clinton. In Auguft, 1777, he was made lieutenant-gen-eral: in 1778, he fucceeded General Howe in the chief command; in June, 1778, he fought at Monmouth; and in December of that year, was appointed colonel of the 84th Royal Highlanders. In April, 1779, he was appointed colonel of the 7th Light Dragoons; in December, failed for Charlefton, which he reduced; and in 1782, returned to England—Sir Guy Carleton fucceeding him in the chief command. He died, December 13, 1795.

INDEX.

24

AUTHORITIES CITED IN THE PRECEDING PAGES.

Autobiography and Correspondence of John Adams.
Bancroft's History of the United States.
Bolton's History of Westchester County.
Booth's History of New York City.
Boston Postboy and Advertiser.
British Army Lists.
Sir Henry Clinton's Narrative and Correspondence.
The Colden Papers. MSS. in the New York Historical Society's Collections.
Collections of the Ulster County Historical Society.
Davis's Memoirs of Aaron Burr.
Dawson's Battles of the United States.
Dawson's The Park and Its Vicinity.
Dawson's Sons of Liberty in New York.
De Voe's MS. Market Book.
Dunlap's History of New York.
Edes and Gill's Boston Gazette.
Force's American Colonial Archives.
Franklin's Works and Correspondence.
Frothingham's Siege of Boston.
Gaine's New York Gazette and the Weekly Mercury.
Gordon's American Revolution.
Graham's History of the United States.
General Heath's Memoirs.
Holt's New York Gazette and Weekly Post-Boy.
Irving's Life of Washington.
Journals of Congress.
Laws of New York.
Leake's Life of General John Lamb.
Memoirs of Charles Lee, Esq.
Lossing's Field Book of the Revolution.
Marshall's Life of George Washington.
Moore's Diary of the American Revolution.
New York Colonial Documents—London Papers.
Ramsay's History of the American Revolution.
Life and Correspondence of Joseph Reed.
Rivington's New York Gazetteer.
Ruttenber's Obstructions to the Navigation of Hudson's River.
Sabine's Sketches of American Loyalists.
Stedman's History of the American War.
Thompson's History of Long Island.
Valentine's Corporation Manual.
Washington's Correspondence, by Sparks.
Watson's Annals and Occurrences of New York City and State.
Willett's Narrative of his Military Actions.